Between Sky and Sea is a story of guilt, loss, and redemption in a world where Native Hawaiian and American cultures collide, causing resentment, confusion, and ultimately, understanding. It's a brilliant rendering of what it means to be Hawaiian, what it means to be family, and what can be the burden, heartbreak, and unbreakable bond of being brothers.
> —**Chris McKinney**, author of *The Tattoo, The Queen of Tears, Bolohead Row, Mililani Mauka*, and *Boi No Good*

Donald Carreira Ching's ability to imbue measured and unsentimental prose with such depth of feeling is the sign of a real talent. Through the perspectives of three brothers in Hawai'i, readers are gifted with a powerful story of how we reconcile ourselves with our land, our culture and the ones we love.
> —**Shawna Yang Ryan**, author of *Water Ghosts* and *Green Island*

By binding us tightly to three brothers occupying very different, sharply invoked spaces in Hawai'i, *Between Sky and Sea* shows us much more than a family's struggle. As we feel the pressures that shape each of these young men, we also come to recognize the relations between people and place, between parents and children, and between desire and duty that make Donald Carreira Ching's first novel a study in intimacy, and a vivid full-length portrait of contemporary Hawai'i. A careful, passionate, and memorable book.
> —**Craig Howes**, Department of English, University of Hawai'i at Mānoa

Between Sky and Sea: A Family's Struggle is about love and despair, about the hardships and rigidities of the human condition. But, ultimately, this is a story about the depth of love and the unfailing beauty of promise, loyalty, and hope. It is a story told by a writer who has an ear sensitive to the voices of our contemporary Local community and to the rhythms of an ancient land tempered by a healing sea.
> —**Gary Pak**, author of *The Watcher of Waipuna, A Ricepaper Airplane, Children of a Fireland, Language of the Geckos, Brothers Under the Same Sky*

In this perspectival account of three brothers, Donald Carreira Ching shows real talent for channeling his characters so thoroughly that he manages to keep out of their way. Reality, this novel of between-ness reminds us, is always far more complex—and far more interesting—than any single version of it.
> —**M. Thomas Gammarino**, author of *Big in Japan* and *Jellyfish Dreams*

Between Sky and Sea
A Family's Struggle

Bamboo Ridge Press

ISBN 978-0-910043-93-9

This is issue #107 (Spring 2015) of *Bamboo Ridge, Journal of Hawai'i Literature and Arts* (ISSN 0733-0308)

Published by Bamboo Ridge Press

Printed in the United States of America

Indexed in *Humanities International Complete*

Bamboo Ridge Press is a member of the Community of Literary Magazines and Presses (CLMP).

Typesetting and design: Rowen Tabusa

Cover photograph: Rowen Tabusa

Author's photograph: Danielle Carreira Ching

Proverbs cited on pages 13, 81, and 133 from Pukui, Mary Kawena. *'Ōlelo No'eau: Hawaiian Proverbs and Poetical Sayings.* Honolulu: Bishop Museum Press, 1983. Print.

Bamboo Ridge Press is a nonprofit, tax-exempt corporation formed in 1978 to foster the appreciation, understanding, and creation of literary, visual, or performing arts by, for, or about Hawai'i's people. This publication was made possible with support from the National Endowment for the Arts (NEA) and the Mayor's Office of Culture and the Arts (MOCA).

Bamboo Ridge is published twice a year. For subscription information, back issues, or a catalog, please contact:

Bamboo Ridge Press
P.O. Box 61781
Honolulu, HI 96839-1781
808.626.1481
brinfo@bambooridge.com
www.bambooridge.com

5 4 3 2 1   15 16 17 18 19

for Danielle Lanakila Carreira Ching

Between Sky and Sea

They were careful to keep to the main channel. Mark avoided the reef while Elani watched the shadowed depths. The moon was hidden behind a bright veil of gray, the light still fell over the ocean in pale stretches, making their path forward clear. When they could make out the strip of sand where the islet split, Mark cut the engine and let the current guide the hull until they were close enough to anchor, Elani hopping out to make sure that the boat was secure.

On the shore, Elani walked up to a spot that faced Kualoa Beach. He looked back at the silhouette of the world that they had left behind and couldn't help but appreciate the quiet. He could hear the breeze, but more than that, he could feel his body pulsing in his ears, echoing with the movement of the waves. He understood now why their brother had been drawn there. Elani could feel its presence in his marrow.

Elani turned back and crossed the sand, climbing up to meet Mark. His brother was waiting for him near a cluster of black rock that protruded up from the ocean, the waves churning below. Elani crouched down and looked out at the ocean. The water was rougher here, deeper.

"I wouldn't have made it," Elani remarked, thinking about how his brothers used to race out to the island when they were kids. "Not out here, not by myself."

"Was some close calls," Mark looked down at his right arm, the scar lost to the hour. "But out hea, we was never alone, ah?"

Elani nodded. "I took that for granted," he licked his lips, tasting the salt air. "All these years."

"No need fo tell me," Mark admitted, stepping out to the edge. "But not tonight," he added. "Not anymore."

They waited until the waves had settled and a thin division of light was on the horizon, with dawn blooming the color of hala flowers. Mark unzipped his backpack and handed one of the bags to his brother. Elani ran his thumb across the plastic, smoothing down the ashes, still not ready to believe that their brother was really gone. "Stay time," he told Elani.

Elani nodded. "Together," he said.

"Fo Kā'eo," Mark added. "Fo Tūtūpapa, fo Pops."

"For all of us," Elani said, and then put the bag between his teeth and slipped down into the water.

Years earlier…

Kāʻeo

Ke hiʻi la ʻoe i ka paukū waena, he neo ke poʻo me ka hiʻu.

You hold the center piece without its head and tail.

Proverb 1696, Pukui 183

E ven Kāʻeo was surprised that he had made it as far as he had. It wasn't that he didn't have the ability for the complexities of Castle High. It was quite the opposite. He had a drive for inquiry and investigation. In fact, he took to questioning his teachers on the value of what he was being taught, but his teachers dismissed his inquiries as irrelevant. So he figured what was the point of working harder than he had to. He decided to get by instead.

He took courses that he knew would be easy. The legendary ones taught by tenured faculty with longstanding nicknames who traded lesson plans for VHS tapes, their attendance books lacking any consistency after the third week of school. He memorized the security shifts, when it was safe to leave campus and when it was okay to return. He knew to always order the two-cheeseburger value meal just in case one of the security guards decided to double-check the back parking lot. He kept track of when the school recording would call his house to let his parents know when he had cut class and erased the messages before they got home. He learned how to forge his mother's handwriting on the notes that he would give to his teachers. And most importantly, he showed up to class frequently enough to keep the principal from reaching out to his parents.

But he couldn't account for everything, specifically Mr. Haywood's junior Language Arts course. It was the only class that Kāʻeo couldn't avoid, Haywood teaching it exclusively that year. Although he had heard stories of the draconian "Mr. Haolewood," Kāʻeo wasn't prepared for Haywood's "Ten Tenets" of proper English or his "Masters" canon of American Literature, most of which Kāʻeo saw no relation to. "What any of dis get fo do wit me?" he had asked. But Mr. Haywood was sure to let Kāʻeo know that his opinion was just that, and it was in his best interests to suck it up and do the work, regardless of his distaste for the material. Kāʻeo thought it was in his best interests to not give a shit what Mr. Haywood thought, and ended up failing the class because of it.

Kāʻeo was proud of the "F," but his mother didn't feel the same. Ma couldn't sleep knowing that her oldest son was turning out to be one of those boys, "da kine everybody whisper about at church."

"Things better change," Ma told him. "No excuses, you understand?" Kāʻeo tried to keep that in mind when the summer session started, but as hard as he tried, he just couldn't deal with Haywood's hour-long lectures on *East of Eden* and other allusions to works by old white men. He lasted a week. "You get all da time in da world fo fool around, ah?" Ma said to him on the drive home from school. "Well, not anymore, you understand? You going spend some time wit your Papa dis summer. Going be good fo you get away, get your head straight."

"But Ma—" he was annoyed. She was well aware of Mr. Haywood's bullshit. She had just listened to him ramble in the principal's office about acceptable behavior and the proper ways that boys Kāʻeo's age should behave. But the arrangement wasn't up for debate.

The next week, Tūtūpapa arrived early to pick Kāʻeo up in his station wagon. He was perpetual beach boy, his uniform the same as it was during his days in Waikīkī: mesh ball-cap, tank top, and blue surf shorts. "Hungry?" Tūtūpapa asked, knowing his grandson well.

They picked up okazu from Kāneʻohe town and then headed back up the coast, stopping at Kualoa Beach Park to split chopsticks and fill their stomachs before spending the rest of the day driving around the island. Kāʻeo had barely finished his shoyu mahi when his grandfather started up. "You know I wen get sent away once fo live wit my aunty. Her husband wen ma-ke and she needed me and my cousins fo do all da kine manini stuffs. Talk about punishment, she never have electricity, she never have clean water. We had fo go down da river fo clean rice." Tūtūpapa stopped to stuff a bite of sweet potato tempura in his mouth. "I tell you, you and your braddahs, you no even know," he mumbled, wiping bits of batter from his beard.

Kāʻeo finished his plate and left his grandfather mid-anecdote to sit in the soft sand and look out at the saltwater playground in front of him. His eyes were fixated on the lone peak in the distance. When he and his little brothers were younger, they would boast about who could reach Chinaman's Hat the fastest, Mark always provoking Kāʻeo with sly slaps to Kāʻeo's stomach, while Elani opted out before the race even began. As they got older and their abilities improved, so did Kāʻeo's and Mark's competitiveness, and Da Race to da Hat became Da Race to da Giant's Toe, a spot so far out on the horizon that Mark had once mistaken a stray buoy for the small toe of the mythical Chinese giant that Tūtūpapa had always said slept beneath the islet. Mark had always joked that the giant was Pordagee—who else you know going try sleep under da water? In his stomach, Kāʻeo could still feel the mix of excitement and anxiety that he had felt each time that they had raced: the rush of the water and the pull of the tide. He would always get back first and sit with his grandfather and Elani and watch the paddlers go out to sea, while he waited for Mark to come in a close second.

"He still down dea you know," Tūtūpapa teased, testing his grandson's memory.

"Nah," Kāʻeo had crossed the water enough times to know better. "Da buggah must be all sand by now," he returned his grandfather's effort anyway.

Tūtūpapa smiled and adjusted his cap, wanting to get a good look at Kāʻeo. "So what, you going tell me what really stay going on wit you or you like me trust what your maddah says?"

"Das what you wen bring me out hea fo, fo lecture me?"

"Nah, but I figgah might as well get um out da way now, ah?" Tūtūpapa mocked Kāʻeo with his eyebrows. "So what, you get one secret girlfriend or something?"

"Nah, nutten li'dat," Kāʻeo resisted. He could have told his grandfather about Haywood, about the lectures he would give to Kāʻeo about his attitude in class or the way that he spoke to him: *This is a classroom, Robert, not your house, not your hale, understand?* Always sure to mistakenly call Kāʻeo by his first name, knowing how much it bothered him. But that wasn't the problem, not really. "I jus no really care about all da bullshit, you know?"

"Like what?" Tūtūpapa was quick. He didn't want to give his

grandson the chance to back out now.

"I dunno," Kāʻeo dismissed the question. The list was too long. "Da kine dey stay teaching us…I no like learn quadratic formulas and read Steinbeck, what dat shit stay good fo anyway?" He looked up in time to see a salt spray shoot up from the rocks in the distance, the waves crashing against the land.

"Das da kine stuffs you need fo know."

"Says who?" Kāʻeo shook his head. "Da teachers too, not like dey get any fucking sense, and not like dey like teach me anyway. Most of dem jus think I get one attitude."

"You in high sku, Kāʻeo, you no get one choice. You go, you do da work, you graduate. You like do something else after, go, but you no can jus drop out. You like end up like my friend Harry Edwards, wen drop out of high sku fo be da next Kui Lee, but guess what, he never realize get one Kui Lee already, now wea you think he stay? Das right, sixty-five, living wit his maddah." Tūtūpapa shook Kāʻeo's shoulder: "Your maddah love you, but I no think she going like you hanging around da house fo dat long."

"You was all right," Kāʻeo looked at the tattoo on his grandfather's shoulder, the hard lines of twin-anchors crossed.

"You like talk about doing shit you no like do, den go ahead, join da military, but guess what, you not going get in witout one diploma or one GED."

"I no like do dat shit either," Kāʻeo said. "Following orders."

"What den?"

"I dunno yet."

"Well, you get time, ah? Jus no waste um," Tūtūpapa added.

"What da hell we waiting fo den?" Kāʻeo asked, slapping his grandfather's shoulder and then heading down to the beach. He left his T-shirt on the sand and ran out to meet the waves. He felt at ease in the water, pushing forward with little effort, not stopping until he reached Chinaman's Hat.

Tūtūpapa was right behind him. He climbed up out of the water. "Wen da hell you wen get so fast?" he asked between breaths. But Kāʻeo was too distracted by his own recollections, his longing for that place. Kāʻeo could hear the coconut trees rustling in the wind, carrying with them names and stories older than the land itself, stories that he didn't know but that he could feel. He climbed higher up. It had been several years, but he was still surprised by the landscape, the plants that overtook the slope, many he didn't recognize. He walked over to a small tree and picked a shriveled orb from between the leaves. "What da fuck?" he asked Tūtūpapa.

"Christmas Berry, pretty but you no like eat dat kine," Tūtūpapa threw it back into the wild. "Maybe das what wen kill da giant, ah?" he added.

Kāʻeo laughed at his grandfather. "You stay jus as nuts as ever, you know dat, Papa?"

"Eh, how you think I wen live dis long?"

"You only part Pordagee?"

"Jus no ask what part," Tūtūpapa threw back with a laugh. "But serious kine, Kāʻeo," Tūtūpapa began, taking advantage of the opportunity while his grandson's guard was down, "stay cuz I wen pay attention, more than jus your eyes and your ears, hea too," he tapped his forehead. "I know you no see any da kine in what dey stay teaching you, but das no excuse, keh?" Tūtūpapa advised. "Cuz you never know, maybe you going need dat kine fo da job you get, or what about wen you get kids, how you going help dem wit their homework? Even if you find out you like learn something else, at least you wen take da chance. No choice still one choice, you understand?"

"Like I wen tell you already," Kāʻeo dodged his grandfather's advice, heading back down to the water. "Get plenny time."

"Jus no waste um," Tūtūpapa repeated his lesson, joining his grandson down at the rocks.

And that was how the rest of Kāʻeo's summer went, the two of them talking story over malasadas or fried rice in the morning, manapua or plate lunch in the afternoon. Between meals, Kāʻeo did his chores: picking weeds from the mondo grass, raking tangerine leaves in the backyard, and mowing the lawn in the front, work that Tūtūpapa could report back to Ma when she called to check in. But most days, his grandfather would order him to put away the bucket, closet the rake, or return the mower back to the garage, and then the two of them would set out. Several days a week, it was for a walk down to the crack seed store on Waiʻalae for rice paper candies and shave ice. Once, it was for a bus trip to Sandy's to watch the surfers when the waves were high. But more often than not, they took an excursion to Waikīkī, where his grandfather would dramatize his teenage years at Queen's Surf to anyone in earshot. It was a welcome break for Kāʻeo, and one that had strengthened the bond that he had with his grandfather.

"What I wen tell you, was good, ah?" Ma asked Kāʻeo when he finally came home in the middle of August. And he had to agree, she had been right. He felt refreshed and invigorated, ready to try again and believing that he could. But what his options were, he wasn't sure.

"The only problem is your Language Arts credit," the counselor pecked at her keyboard. "It looks like you can drop one of your electives and pick up the one you're missing." She reached into her desk and pulled out a class listing. Her finger ran down the line-up. Kāʻeo leaned over, watching her acrylic nail stop at Haywood's name and then move past it. "You're quite the student," she said, glancing up at his academic record.

"No worry," he told her. "Das not going be one problem anymore."

She looked at the class listing again. "Ms. Carvalho," she looked up. Kāʻeo didn't recognize the name. "From what I hear, the class is challenging but different."

Different, he wasn't sure about that. "Get anybody else?" he asked.

The counselor threw Kāʻeo a half smile. "Different's good," she assured him, signing with swift, black strokes from her pen. He hoped that she was right.

On the first day, Kāʻeo didn't know what to expect. When he got to the room, he found the seats were organized in a circle and the desk Ms. Carvalho sat in was no different than the others. She began class by talking about the power of words and about how stories can shape how writers view themselves and the world that they live in. "Stories are everywhere," she exclaimed to the class, "especially here in Hawaiʻi, with much of the islands' histories rooted in story." Kāʻeo looked around him, not sure if he was in the right place. "Which brings us to our first assignment," she stood up, and chalked the guidelines on the board.

"Each of you is required to research and report on a significant place here on Oʻahu," she continued. "It's important for you to choose a place that you're familiar with, but also one that you're interested in learning more about."

The rest of their class time was spent free writing and brainstorming ideas. Kāʻeo did his best to use Ms. Carvalho's pre-writing strategies, but found that he still couldn't generate a topic that met her criteria. Then, on the bus ride home from school, Kāʻeo looked out the window and saw Chinaman's Hat set against streaks of deep red. He thought about Tūtūpapa's giant, and wondered if there was more of a history there than just his grandfather's frayed yarn.

What he found surprised him. Chinaman's Hat wasn't a hat at all, it was Mokoliʻi, the tip of a giant lizard's tail. At the library, he read about Pele and her sister Hiʻiakaikapoliopele, who had broken the back of the creature. A "moʻo," Kāʻeo said the word aloud. He borrowed all of the books that he could find on the islet and spent his whole weekend writing his report.

When he got his grade back the following week, he was quick to leave it on the kitchen counter for his family to see. "Eh, must be one mistake or something," Mark remarked when he saw it. "Get your name on dis."

"No ack," Kāʻeo grabbed the paper from him. "You da one going have fo repeat your freshman year, you dumbass."

"I not you," Mark joked.

"Das my point," Kāʻeo got the last word in. "Dipshit."

"You like chili pepper?" Ma scolded them.

"Let me take a look," their father reached for the paper. "You did all this research yourself?"

"Das right," Kāʻeo was still excited by his grade. "Stay crazy how all da names get one story behind them," he began to tell them. "All da places get one connection, you know? And das how was, das how stay," he corrected himself. "Wen you know da history, you know how everything comes together." Kāʻeo began to tell them about the moʻolelo of Pele and her sister, at least what little he knew.

Elani was intrigued. "It's like a Greek myth," he added, lifting his head up from his book.

Kāʻeo wasn't sure how to explain it to his brother. "Sort of," he replied, not wanting to crush his brother's interest.

Ma was proud. "I dunno what wen get into you," she told him, "but no let up, keh?"

"I no get time fo waste," he replied, remembering his grandfather's words.

Over the next two months, the class had gone from writing reports on place to analyzing literature written about Hawaiʻi, fiction and non-fiction alike. He was engaged and focused, even more so when he found out about their next assignment: an oral history of a family member or friend. Ms. Carvalho guided the class to compose a script for when they interviewed the person they chose, and also let them know that they would be responsible for "fact-checking," researching the historical details. "Remember that there needs to be some significance to the person you choose. Think about your audience: why would they be interested in reading about your subject?" Tūtūpapa had fought in Vietnam, he had owned his own restaurant, and he had more stories than anyone else that Kāʻeo knew. The choice was an easy one.

But when Kāʻeo suggested to his grandfather that he spend Thanksgiving break with him to work on it, Tūtūpapa was apprehensive. "Dis not really one good time," Tūtūpapa told him over the phone. He didn't understand. When Ma found out about Tūtūpapa's reaction, she grew concerned too, her bewilderment triggered by a logic that Kāʻeo was unaware of. She immediately called Tūtūpapa back and made plans to have Thanksgiving dinner at his house.

"I no care," Ma told him over the phone. "We going be dea, you understand?"

It was a tense affair. They arrived at Tūtūpapa's house only to find that he wasn't home. When he did show up, half an hour later than he was supposed to, he was hurried and flushed, a flood of sandalwood cologne reeking from his collar, a turkey dinner from Zippy's in one hand, and his keys fumbling in the other.

"What da hell stay going on wit you?" Ma asked Tūtūpapa after dinner. The two of them were in the kitchen cleaning up. Kāʻeo was out on the lānai with his brothers: Mark and Elani fighting over the remote, while Kāʻeo listened to his mother and grandfather through the screen door. "You no think I can smell da kine on your breath?"

"Das nutten," Tūtūpapa stalled. "I wen go church," he finally said. "Wen take communion, das all."

"You think I one fool?" Ma asked. "I wen see da news, I know about Danny boy."

Kāʻeo strained to hear the rest of their conversation but his brothers were too loud. "Give me da fucking remote already," Mark had Elani pinned to the ground. "Nobody but you like watch dis dorky shit."

"Get off of me," Elani tried to push Mark off, but he was no match for his brother's girth.

"What da hell stay wrong wit you?" Kāʻeo grabbed Mark and pulled him off of Elani. "You stupid or what, leave him alone already. Nobody like watch your bullshit either, dumbass."

"Eh, guess who wen ask you?" Mark joked, reaching for the remote.

Kāʻeo grabbed it first and turned off the television. "I think both you babies need some fucking time to yourselves." Elani wiped his eyes and walked away without a word. Mark glared at Kāʻeo. "You get one problem?" Kāʻeo tempted Mark. Mark mumbled under his breath and retreated inside the house.

Pops was at the screen door. He held it open for Kāʻeo. "We're leaving," Pops told him.

Kāʻeo was confused. He walked inside. Ma and Tūtūpapa had disappeared from the kitchen, but he could hear them down the hall, their voices growing louder. "Everything okay?" he asked his father.

"I've got a long shift tomorrow and we need to get you guys home," Pops explained.

"What about Papa?" Kāʻeo asked. "I still need fo do my interview wit him."

"Your grandfather needs some time," Ma said, walking out from the hallway. "Can talk to him tomorrow."

"I stay hea already."

"Tomorrow," she told Kāʻeo, leaving him no room to argue.

But tomorrow came and went, and Kāʻeo was anxious to get started and concerned about his grandfather's well being. "Your Papa not feeling well right now, Kāʻeo," Ma told him, "das all." He didn't buy it. And when Kāʻeo asked his father about what Ma had told him, Pops told him the same thing. "Let your mother handle it," he advised.

Kāʻeo could hear Ma in his voice. "Handle what?" Kāʻeo asked.

Pops realized his mistake. "Nothing," he said, dismissing Kāʻeo's inquiry.

Bullshit, Kāʻeo thought. He would find out for himself.

When the weekend came, Kāʻeo woke up early and took the 85A to St. Louis, and walked the rest of the way to his grandfather's house. Kāʻeo rang the doorbell and waited. He rang it one more time before he heard the deadbolt release and his grandfather opened the door just enough to peek out from behind it. He saw a sliver of his face. "Your maddah know you hea?" Tūtūpapa asked.

It was a strange question. "No," Kāʻeo said, not sure how else to respond.

Tūtūpapa nodded and opened the door for his grandson. "You wen eat already?" he asked Kāʻeo.

"I'm good," Kāʻeo said. He walked around the dining room and scanned the living room. He could tell by the water rings on the table and the Bible on his grandfather's recliner that Tūtūpapa had been staying in, but when he looked at his grandfather he saw no sign that he was ill. He didn't know what Ma was talking about. "You doing okay?" Kāʻeo asked just to be sure.

"I doing fine." Tūtūpapa brought two glasses of ice water from the kitchen.

Kāʻeo dropped his script on the table and picked up his glass. He swirled the ice around, listening to the cubes clink when they rose and hit the side. "Did you know about Hiʻiaka?" Kāʻeo asked. He didn't know why, but he was nervous. "Did you know dat Chinaman's Hat stay Mokoliʻi's tail?" He felt like he was a kid again, waiting for permission to ask the questions that he wanted to.

His grandfather shook his head, the moʻolelo foreign to him. "Dis what you wen come all dis way fo?"

Kāʻeo flashed a quick smile and reached for the script. "I get one report fo do," Kāʻeo explained. "One oral history, you no remember?"

"Das right, das right," Tūtūpapa nodded.

"Cool, cool," Kāʻeo looked over the questions. "What you and Ma was arguing about da oddah night?" he blurted out.

Tūtūpapa opened his mouth to speak but then stopped himself. "Maybe you like hear about da restaurant? I ever tell you about da one time my friend Jimmy Bautista…" Tūtūpapa began, placing his cup down on the bare table, a bead of sweat falling down the glass.

"Ma said you was sick or something," Kāʻeo shook his head. "But you no look sick to me."

"You know how your maddah stay," Tūtūpapa reasoned with Kāʻeo. "She jus da kine, you know?"

"Das what I wen tell her too, but she still wen ack like shit was serious or something. She never like tell me nutten and I was starting fo think something was up between you guys."

"Like what?" Tūtūpapa said quickly.

"I dunno," Kāʻeo asked, picking up his glass again. "Pops wen tell me fo let Ma handle things."

"Handle what?"

"Exactly," Kāʻeo looked at his grandfather, waiting for him to break. "And I stay da kine too though, tripping cuz you never like me come over hea, and den Ma wen get all nuts about Thanksgiving, and den you guys was fighting in da kitchen—"

"We was talking," Tūtūpapa admitted. "Das all."

"You guys was arguing, Papa," Kāʻeo said. "And den we had fo leave, and I never even get one chance fo talk to you about my sku stuffs, about how good I stay doing, or about my new teacher, you know, she stay one trip, Papa, nutten like Haolewood. She wen tell da class dat we need fo read and write about da kine dat affects us most."

"Tell me," Tūtūpapa said, bringing his chair closer to his grandson.

Kāʻeo shook his head. "You first," he bartered with his grandfather.

"I dunno what fo tell you," Tūtūpapa replied.

"Da truth," Kāʻeo said honestly. "Why Ma was all piss off wit you? Why everybody acking like nutten stay going? Why everybody get excuses?"

"You're persistent, you know dat?"

"I jus like know what stay going on, Papa," Kāʻeo assured him. "I jus worried about you."

Tūtūpapa clasped his hands in his lap and looked at his grandson. "I think maybe your maddah…"

"Papa," Kāʻeo interjected. "I not one kid anymore, you know dat, right?"

Tūtūpapa nodded. "Between us den, ah?"

"I not going say nutten," Kāʻeo promised.

Tūtūpapa took his time. "I not going ack like I always wen make da best choices in life, you know?" Tūtūpapa said, finding his way between pauses. "Stay like my friend, Stanton Ching, da first thing he wen do wen he got out da military was hit da bar. Wen he was out of work or wen he had one hard time, da first thing he wen do was sit on da couch wit one six-pack." Tūtūpapa searched the table with his eyes. "Das why hard sometimes, you understand? Can try fo keep moving in da right direction, but no stay dat easy, ah?" He shook his head, realizing his mistake. "Not like das one excuse."

Kāʻeo was lost. "One excuse fo what?" he replied, trying to decipher what his grandfather was struggling to tell him. He thought about what his mother had yelled at Tūtūpapa, *You no think I can smell da kine on your breath.* "You acking like you stay one alcoholic or something, Papa," Kāʻeo meant it as a joke, but he saw the look on his grandfather's face and realized that he was the only one smiling.

Tūtūpapa took a breath. "Sometimes da kine get in da way, you know? Sometimes stay small kine stuffs, manini bullshit, you understand? But da small stuff, only stay small so long, den da buggah build and build."

"Like one wave," Kāʻeo finished his grandfather's metaphor, finding himself unable to focus on anything else.

"Das right," Tūtūpapa replied. "And sometimes, you know, can handle, and sometimes no can, you understand?"

Kāʻeo nodded, afraid to open his mouth and let the rush of questions out. "You okay?" he finally asked.

"I doing alright fo now," Tūtūpapa told Kāʻeo. "Was doing good fo one long time."

"Something wen happen between you and Ma?" Kāʻeo asked,

pacing his inquiry.

"Me and my braddah," Tūtūpapa clarified. "Your Uncle Joseph."

"I never know you had one braddah," he didn't hide his surprise.

"He wen pass away long time ago, befo you was born, befo your maddah was born even," Tūtūpapa explained. "Small kid time," Tūtūpapa smiled, "was like how you and Mark stay, always trying fo get da upper hand on each oddah, always trying fo get my faddah's attention. But you know, wen he wen get older, he was very, you know," Tūtūpapa placed his hands on either side of his face and narrowed his vision. "Was one way or no way, fo him, maybe fo da both of us." Tūtūpapa took a drink of water, his throat dry. "He jus wen have one fire in him." Tūtūpapa took another sip, his hands shaking, the ice tinkling. "You too young fo know, but plenny was going on den, yah? Your uncle jus wanted fo make one difference, you understand? He never like da kine dat was going on and he wanted fo change things. Das our responsibility," Tūtūpapa said, channeling the memory. "Das what he always wen say to me."

"What was?" Kāʻeo asked.

"Fo fight fo be Hawaiian," Tūtūpapa explained, doing his best to be as clear as he could be. "Fo fight fo Hawaiʻi."

The wind came through the jalousies. Kāʻeo felt it run down his spine. "And what, you never agree wit him?"

"I live in da real world," Tūtūpapa looked away from his grandson and out the picture window. "I never have time fo waste. I needed fo work, you know? Fo provide fo him and my maddah after our faddah wen ma-ke. Das *my* responsibility, I wen tell him, but he jus wanted fo hold his signs and fool around, and den wen he wen get Lei pregnant," Tūtūpapa shook his head. At that moment, Kāʻeo wasn't sure if his grandfather was talking to him or to himself. "You get one responsibility to Danny boy now, das what I told him. But still he never like listen, even after he wen get himself arrested he wen ack all da kine. So I wen do what I wen have fo do, regardless of what he wen think. Wen family no take care, you take care, you know?" Tūtūpapa brought his fingers to his chest and felt the crucifix under his shirt.

"Danny boy," Kāʻeo repeated, recalling the name.

"Das your cousin," Tūtūpapa confirmed. "Your second cousin

really," he took a breath. "He wen ma-ke in one car accident last month. I never see him or his maddah long time, and den fo hear about him li'dat," Tūtūpapa took a breath. "Life jus stay hard sometimes, you know? And sometimes can get da better of you. I not proud of how I wen ack, but I get things under control now, and your maddah knows dat, but she still like worry about me. And wen she wen hear about what wen happen to your cousin."

"You jus wen need time," Kā'eo replied, wondering if there was more to the story than Tūtūpapa was letting on.

"I wen hear da news and den everything else when start fo hit me, das all. But I doing okay now, yah, and things going settle down, I promise." He looked over at Kā'eo's notes, at the blank page. "So what?" Tūtūpapa asked, ready to bring the topic to a close. "You like get dis thing done wit or what?"

Kā'eo nodded in understanding and reached for the script, flipping to the first page. "You was saying something about da restaurant and your friend?"

"Jimmy Bautista," Tūtūpapa tapped the table, switching gears. "Man, he was one character, I tell you."

They spent the rest of the morning talking story about Tūtūpapa's life: about his time in the Navy, about when he had met Kā'eo's grandmother, and about the restaurant that they had opened together. Kā'eo had filled his script to the margins and knew that he had what he needed to complete his assignment, but when he got up to tell his grandfather goodbye, he knew that he had other questions that he hadn't asked and that he wanted to. Questions about his granduncle and about that sense of responsibility that had divided them. But he knew better than to push.

Kā'eo embraced his grandfather. "Wait hea, keh?" Tūtūpapa told him, squeezing his grandson's shoulders. He left Kā'eo and went into his bedroom. When he came back, he had an old cigar box in his hand. "No tell your maddah you wen come hea," Tūtūpapa told him, handing him the box. "I no like you get in trouble."

"I no understand," Kā'eo said, looking at the box. He went for the lid but Tūtūpapa reached it first.

"Not now," Tūtūpapa said, walking his grandson to the door. "You can get home okay?"

"Yah, I get one bus pass," Kāʻeo said, slipping the box into his backpack.

"You call if you need me come get you, okay?"

Kāʻeo looked up at his grandfather, he could tell that their conversation had weighed on him. "You going be alright?"

"One day at a time," Tūtūpapa reassured his grandson, the two of them sharing another embrace.

"Jus no waste um right?" Kāʻeo told him, squeezing his grandfather back.

While Kāʻeo worked on the draft of his paper, he kept a photograph pinned to the corkboard behind his computer; a picture that he had found in the box that Tūtūpapa had given him. It was of his grandfather and another man, who Kāʻeo guessed was his granduncle, standing with their backs against a run-down boat. He was surprised at the contrast, his granduncle smaller in stature but leaner, his face more defined, and rather than the close-cut that Tūtūpapa wore, his granduncle's hair fell in an untamed mass down past his naked shoulders. They were smiling, but his granduncle kept his teeth hidden and his focus was contemplative and reserved; whereas Tūtūpapa held nothing back, flashing every inch of white and throwing a shaka to the camera's lens.

By the year on the back of the image, Kāʻeo guessed that Tūtūpapa must have been around his age, maybe a few years older, not yet enlisted, but already Kāʻeo could see the division between them. And as much as Kāʻeo recognized his grandfather, he also realized how little he knew about Tūtūpapa and about his life, and in that way both men were strangers to him. Half-truths that made Kāʻeo wonder about his own life and about who he was. So when he was finally finished with his essay, he wasn't surprised to find that his paper was filled with more questions than answers. An interrogation of a history that he thought he knew.

Even after Kāʻeo turned his assignment in, he continued his research. While he learned about Waiāhole, Kalama Valley, and Kahoʻolawe, he talked to his mother about Tūtūpapa's life before the war and after, and she gave him slivers of his grandfather's past: that Tūtūpapa had been real kolohe when he was growing up, that his father had died when he was still in high school, and that he had enlisted to take care of his family, though she failed to mention what had happened to them when he returned. Noting instead that he loved his mother and his brother: "Family stay everything to your Papa."

"What wen happen between dem?" Kāʻeo asked Ma, a detail that both his mother and Tūtūpapa had left out. "Wit Papa and Uncle Joseph."

"Nutten," Ma was quick to reply, the name catching her off guard. "Dey jus wen lose touch, das all," she said, and with Tūtūpapa's admittance and explanation, it was enough for Kāʻeo to at least understand why it was such a difficult topic for his grandfather to talk about and why no one had ever brought it up before.

His interests soon turned inward. Kāʻeo asked about where his name had come from, and he learned that his grandmother's father had been named Kāʻeo. And that they had gotten Kāʻeo's first name, Robert, from Tūtūpapa's father. "Wen your Papa was growing up, was good fo have one first name li'dat. Need fo have one first name li'dat," she added. When Kāʻeo asked her why, "Cuz das jus how things was back den," was her only response. And by the time New Year's came around and Tūtūpapa came over to help Ma prepare the vinha d'alhos, Kāʻeo no longer had to wonder why the house always smelled like vinegar for the first three days of January, or why Tūtūpapa had only told Kāʻeo and his brothers about the pale giant that had fallen asleep in Kāneʻohe Bay. Those were the only stories that his grandfather had known, but Kāʻeo wanted more than just shallow traditions and local color, he wanted to understand himself as his granduncle had. He wanted to understand what it meant to be from Hawaiʻi, not just from Hawaii, and he knew that it was a lesson that Tūtūpapa could never teach him.

By the time school started up again, Kāʻeo was nervous about his paper. There was so much more that he had learned over the break, and he wanted more than anything to have another chance at writing it. After class, he explained to Ms. Carvalho how he felt, but she assured him that it was fine. "I would rather you save your effort for the next assignment," she told him. "But while you're here, there's an opportunity I want you to think about, a scholarship that I think you might be interested in." She took a manila envelope off of her desk and handed it to Kāʻeo. "There's a matter of the personal narrative and the forms to fill out, but after reading your essay, I think you'd make an excellent candidate. The college has a great Hawaiian Studies program, and I think you'd really enjoy it."

"I dunno. I no really get one good record, you know?"

"You've made a lot of strides this year," Ms. Carvalho assured him. "Don't doubt yourself."

College? The thought still seemed out of reach. "I no really..."

"In your essay, you said you wanted answers, right?" she asked Kāʻeo, and he did. "Well, here's your chance," she told him, and he took the envelope, wanting more than anything to find out for himself.

The first time had only taken a few minutes. Kāʻeo had finished one cup and was running his tongue over his gums while he listened intently to his professor, Dr. Kauhane, lecture him and a group of other students about the drink that they were sharing during the extra credit workshop. " ʻawa was one of the first plants that was brought over with the Polynesians," she lectured. "Medicinally, it has a variety of applications: it can be used to treat weariness, asthma, and even arthritis. It can be used as a sedative, to relax the muscles and the mind," she pointed to her forehead as she circled her students. "Its sacredness is also emphasized in moʻolelo and it has ceremonial importance as well, the ʻawa bowl often shared in celebration and camaraderie, but also in thanks to the gods and the ʻāina, from which all knowledge is gained." She paused, "And yet as significant as ʻawa is, it is seen by some as an intoxicant, which is why after missionaries arrived, the planting of ʻawa was looked down upon and later forbidden."

"How the hell did you talk me into this?" Kāʻeo's friend Alakaʻi Hee whispered to him. Theirs was a friendship developed from proximity and coincidence, two people who had found themselves in the same courses again and again. Alakaʻi's background differed greatly from Kāʻeo's: Alakaʻi had graduated from Kamehameha; he was fluent in Hawaiian; and, Alakaʻi bragged, one of his ancestors was a master navigator, though Kāʻeo wasn't sure what difference it really made. Alakaʻi showed fervor in the political and social debates that often drove the discussions in other courses, but for all his impassioned discourse, he rarely put forth any effort into his work.

"You need the extra points," Kāʻeo reminded him, annoyed with his interruption.

"Today," Dr. Kauhane glanced in their direction, "you will be preparing the drink in the traditional way. First, you will clean the root, then slice it into small pieces, chewing them and then pounding them with water before straining the result," she continued. "You may also try cutting and chewing larger chunks; a few pieces in the mouth should give you the desired effect." One of his other classmates, Chloe Foster, had already begun to work. Kāʻeo was sitting across from her, watching her wash the root. He had taken a few seminar courses with her, but had never really gotten the chance, or the courage, to make his approach. Alakaʻi leaned in to add his own commentary, but Dr. Kauhane was quick. "Ua maopopo iāʻoe?" she asked, snapping her fingers near his ear.

"E kala mai," Alakaʻi apologized.

"Sorry," Kāʻeo added. The rest of his classmates laughed. Chloe just smiled at him and returned to her work. Kāʻeo caught her gaze.

"I get it now," Alakaʻi said, softer this time. "No worries, I got you."

"What?" Kāʻeo matched his tone. "No," he said, realizing what Alakaʻi was up to.

But Alakaʻi ignored him and finished his cup, suddenly inspired, saving the punch line for after the session was dismissed. Alakaʻi stood near his ʻawa bowl and waited. When Chloe walked by, he was quick to ask her opinion. "So me and my friend are hoping you can give us some insight," he told her, holding Kāʻeo against his will. "Sorry, my name's Kaʻi by the way and this is Kāʻeo, you guys have met right?"

"Chloe," she said, giving him a small wave, "I think we've had a couple of classes together." Kāʻeo was surprised that she had remembered. "So what's going on?" she asked.

"Taste this," Alakaʻi offered her a cup, "and tell us what you think I've done wrong."

She took it, staring down at the pieces of bark floating on the surface.

"Everything," she laughed, not even bothering to take a sip.

Kāʻeo saw his opportunity, taking the bark water out of her hands and handing her a helping of his. "He dunno what he doing," Kāʻeo quipped.

"You're right," she complimented Kāʻeo, tipping the cup toward her lips. "This is perfect."

"Eh, at least give mine a chance," Alakaʻi said, taking his cup and knocking it back. Alakaʻi retched. "On second thought," he smiled and dumped the remaining portion back in the bowl.

"A good effort though," she conceded out of courtesy.

"Not at all," Alakaʻi added, the three of them sharing a laugh.

And that's how it began, a casual affair at first. They met up at Dr. Kauhane's for the extra credit sessions and stayed afterwards to talk story. Chloe was a year older than the both of them, double majoring in Ethnic Studies and Hawaiian Studies. Much like Alakaʻi, she found herself drawn to discussions of colonialism and ideology. Not one to be to outdone, Kāʻeo would throw in what he remembered regarding Marxist theory, commodity fetishism, and cultural appropriation, but eventually Alakaʻi's expertise and enthusiasm for the subject matter would overcome Kāʻeo's attempts at engagement. Once, he even attempted to bring up his granduncle's activist past, but when Chloe voiced her interest, Kāʻeo found himself lacking in the details that she was looking for.

As the weeks went on, Chloe and Alakaʻi's debates became playful flirtations that echoed in the halls or on the way to their cars. They lingered in the parking lot until Kāʻeo grew tired and left the two of them alone. It was clear what was going on in front of him, and although he wished the circumstances were different, he was fine with it. But then things began to change.

It was the last day of the semester, the weekly meeting had been cancelled but Dr. Kauhane had asked the three of them to meet her anyway. Of everyone who had attended her extra credit sessions, Kāʻeo, Chloe, and Alakaʻi had been the only ones who had shown up consistently. When Kāʻeo got there, he found Chloe and Dr. Kauhane in the classroom, the two of them sharing a bowl of ʻawa. "Just the person we were looking for," Dr. Kauhane remarked.

"We not in trouble or nutten, right?" Kāʻeo laughed.

"It's nothing like that," she said. "I was just telling Chloe that I have a job for the two of you, if you folks are interested. It doesn't pay much, but the experience can be quite rewarding."

Kāʻeo gave Chloe a look, trying to discern the nature of the job from her face. She had a glow about her today, the natural browns and auburns of her hair making her eyes flicker. "One job?" Kāʻeo asked. "Like one T.A. or something?"

"Not quite," Dr. Kauhane replied. "I have a small plot of land behind my house in Waikāne. My mother used to grow quite a bit there, but since I've moved back from Hawaiʻi Island, I really haven't had the time to work on it."

"She wants to know if we'd be interested in growing ʻawa there," Chloe added, filling Kāʻeoʼs cup.

"Among other indigenous plants," Dr. Kauhane explained. "ʻAla ʻala wai nui, palapalai, māmaki. If possible, I'd like to eventually make it a place where students can practice what they learn here as well as provide materials for the work in my other classes."

"Fo real?" Kāʻeo took the cup from Chloe. He loved the idea, especially with summer on the horizon.

"Lawe i ka maʻalea a kūʻonoʻono," Dr. Kauhane said, waiting for either of them to recognize the proverb.

"Acquire skill and make it deep," Chloe remembered.

"What about Alakaʻi?" Kāʻeo asked, suddenly aware of his absence.

"What about him?" Chloe replied, raising her cup. "You know how he feels about this kind of thing."

Kāʻeo wasn't going to argue her point. "E hō mai," he said, unable to hold his excitement in. He knew the experience would be one to remember, and spending more time with Chloe wouldn't hurt.

They got to work a weekend later, the two of them clearing the brush and preparing the soil. Dr. Kauhane had a friend who owned a farm in Waimānalo, which gave Kāʻeo and Chloe the opportunity to transplant a few older plants while they nurtured and cared for the younger roots. Kāʻeo couldn't help but feel an overwhelming sense of calm when he was there, and he often found himself exploring past the boundaries of Dr. Kauhaneʼs land. After his work was done, he would sometimes walk down to the stream that ran below the cottage or follow its length up into the mountain, climbing until he found a spot high enough to see over the trees and down to Mokoliʻi. It was at those times that he felt the most at peace.

But when Chloe was there, she was all he needed. Rather than explore their surroundings, she would take a break from their labor and seek comfort inside the cottage. Oftentimes, she would bring niu leaf or lauhala and practice the many weaving techniques that she was learning in one of her other classes, working to balance her analytical nature through the discipline. She was skilled with the material, and took to teaching Kāʻeo, taking his hands and showing him how to fold the pieces into place. Kāʻeo sensed something more in her movements, but he did his best to focus on the work, while Chloe lectured him on why she felt so connected to what they were doing.

"It's how you keep the knowledge alive," she told him one day, laying the material in thick double wefts. "I know my parents never took the time with me and I wish they had, you know? Guess they didn't understand the importance of this kind of education." Kāʻeo had given up on following her lead and moved to one of the tables to work on his ʻōlelo Hawaiʻi. "What was it for you?" she asked him.

"Stay cuz I never really have one education liʻdis either," he answered honestly. "Was always math, science, English. Was always da kine teaching I never wen connect wit or anada person's story dat never get shit fo do wit me." He paused and let his experience link with his studies. "Fo me was like every time I wen look through dat Western lens, I wen feel blind," he added, hoping to impress her.

"What about your uncle?" she asked, her attention sparked.

"Like I wen tell you," Kāʻeo answered. "My Papa and my uncle never really see eye to eye, ah? From what I know, my uncle was like us, trying fo understand how things stay, trying fo make one difference, and my Papa, he was jus trying fo keep things going, fo take care da family. My uncle was out dea fighting and my Papa wen join da Navy," he left out the consequence of their divide. "My uncle was gone long time before I was born, so no one really wen talk about him either. And everybody else, dat whole side of da family, all of dem ma-ke or someplace else, scattered liʻdat. Was always jus me, my parents, my braddahs, and my Papa, but none of dem really understand any of dis either," Kāʻeo said, surveying the room. "No one I know does," he looked at her. Even me sometimes, he wanted to say, but he was too ashamed to admit it even though he knew that she could relate.

"You're not alone," she replied without restraint.

"I guess das why we stay hea, ah?" Kāʻeo replied. "Fo learn, fo understand, fo try fo get one sense of da kine we never have. And I like dis, you know? Doing something dat matters, das about our culture." Dirt from his fingers had made its way to the page of his notebook. He looked at his palms: the caked pathways that lined them. "Our truths stay right hea in da stories and in da land. Stay like one part of ourselves we can hold, you know? On our tongues and in our hands," he added.

"It's your kuleana," she said, in tune with his reflection. "Your responsibility to who you are." He nodded. "A rhetoric of resistance," Chloe continued, more serious than he expected. "You're doing something real, you know? It might not change the world, but in some small way it does."

"I know dat," he admitted, closing his notebook. "Feels good too, you know? Fo have one part in da process. Can see myself doing something li'dis too. Not jus ʻawa though, maybe can learn oddah stuffs. Kalo li'dat, start one loʻi. Like you said, maybe das my kuleana, ah? Fo make one difference in my own way, you know?"

"That's the only way you can, right?" she added, complimenting his sentiment.

"I dunno," he laughed at the thought of his own acreage. The cost of land alone would be monumental. "Eventually I going figgah um out."

"You just got to keep doing what you're doing," she said, reaching for his hand.

He could feel a heat bubbling up his chest. "I going be right back," he said, sure that he would soak his shirt through if he stayed.

Kāʻeo went back behind the cottage, to the ʻawa patch. He touched the soil with his hands, the earth still soft from the bouts of rainfall that they had been having. He walked around the small patch, picking out weeds that he had missed, occasionally looking up through the treetops for a glimpse of sun. When he was done, he went back inside and began to prepare one of the older roots, Chloe joining him at the sink, and for a brief moment their bodies were working as one.

They spent the rest of that summer together but apart. A relationship of necessity, built on cooperation and mutual purposes. There were glimmers of intimacy, or so Kāʻeo thought, and thus he continued to sow the space between them. Progress was slow but consistent. On several occasions, they left their work early to have lunch, and there was even talk of making it a standing appointment in the fall. They talked about the future—Chloe's plans for grad school and Kāʻeo's class schedule for the next year—and the past, with Kāʻeo leaving nothing out when it came to his relationships: fourteen-day romances and peer-pressure couplings included.

Although Chloe was more than willing to divulge embarrassing details about her intermediate school crushes and prom night mishaps, the subject of her relationship with Alakaʻi was a matter that she cared to leave unaddressed. Kāʻeo was patient but had his limits, and so one day over a plate of lūʻau stew, he asked her about Alakaʻi directly, hoping that it would give him the opportunity to make his intentions known. "Stay over between you two or what?" he asked, but she ignored the question and replied with distance instead.

"Does it matter?" Chloe replied, making it clear exactly where she stood.

It wasn't long after that day that Kāʻeo arrived at the cottage to find Chloe at the edge of the ʻawa patch on the phone, laughing and speaking in hushed tones. When he asked her about it, she dismissed his inquiry: "No one," she said, and then went inside to weave, knowing that Kāʻeo would be working outside for much of the day. Soon, it was more than just phone calls. She began to neglect her work, not arriving until later in the day or missing scheduled trips to the farm supply. Then, with August only a week away, Kāʻeo decided to show up early to tend the ʻawa patch and go for a hike, and ended up stumbling upon Chloe and Alakaʻi touring the grounds, their hands only inches apart.

"What da hell you doing out hea?" Kāʻeo asked, trying to hold back his insecurity.

Alakaʻi beamed and moved to embrace Kāʻeo. "I just came to check out what I've been missing," he said.

"Plenny," Kāʻeo shot back, stepping to the side.

"I can tell," Alakaʻi said, nodding at the meager ʻawa stalks. "You guys did a great job." Kāʻeo was sure he was being sarcastic.

"Stay more," Kāʻeo defended. "We get plenny ʻahuʻawa down by da stream. Get palapalai on da oddah side."

"Are you going to tell him?" Chloe asked Alakaʻi, Kāʻeo recognizing the excitement on her face.

"Tell me what?"

"What he's been doing this whole time," she added.

"It's nothing," Alakaʻi dismissed Chloe's inquiry, his humility surprising Kāʻeo.

"Nothing?" Chloe laughed. "You know the protests at the construction site downtown?" Chloe asked Kāʻeo.

"Over da iwi dey wen dig up?" Kāʻeo asked. Chloe nodded.

"I'm not doing much, just helping with the organization," Alakaʻi replied. "But when I found out that I had family buried there, well…"

"You just had to act," Chloe smiled, her fingers dancing down his arm.

"Bullshit." Kāʻeo couldn't believe it. In all the time that Kāʻeo had been friends with Alakaʻi, Kāʻeo had never known him to work harder than he had to. He couldn't count the number of times that they had been grouped together for projects, with Kāʻeo having to shoulder most of the responsibility. "You telling me you actually get your shit together fo once?"

"I get it, you're pissed I left you guys to do all this by yourselves," Alakaʻi replied. "But you know how I am about this kind of stuff, I just don't get it, you know?"

Kāʻeo clenched his fist. "But I'm here because I want to make up for it. I'm holding a planning session tonight and I want you two to join us."

Kāʻeo wasn't buying it. "Sorry, no disrespect, you know? But I no like waste my time wit your half-ass bullshit."

"I know it's last minute, but we could really use your support out there," Alakaʻi wrangled Kāʻeo's shoulders and pulled him close. "We need your passion." Kāʻeo was sure that Alakaʻi was mocking him now.

"It'll be good," Chloe encouraged Kāʻeo, taking the bait. "Imagine the difference we could make."

Kāʻeo pushed Alakaʻi hard. "I stay making one difference already," he told her and walked away. "More than dis fuckah ever did anyway."

He didn't bother waiting to say goodbye to Alakaʻi. Instead, he went down to the river and watched the crayfish jitter across the rocks. He remembered toying with them as a kid down by the stream near his house, picking them up and throwing them at his brothers or pretending to smash them with heavy stones. Although he knew better now, he couldn't help but feel the urge to pick one up and play god with it again, separating its life from its shell.

"Are you okay?" Chloe asked him a short time later. He heard her coming down the trail but hadn't bothered to greet her. He was glad to see that she was alone.

"Fuck him," Kāʻeo was blunt, his eyes on a large crayfish that had just emerged from the water. "He thinks he can jus show up and ack like he stay one fucking superhero or something, like he wen fucking put one stop to da cranes down dea, but I no buy dat shit. He dunno what real work about."

"Maybe he's changed," Chloe suggested, crouching down beside Kāʻeo.

Kāʻeo grabbed the crayfish and held it up on its back. "Nah," he told her. "Dis about something else, ah?"

"Like what?"

"You tell me," Kāʻeo prodded, watching the crayfish's limbs thrash helplessly. "All summer you never say one fucking word about whatever wen happen between da two of you, and now Hawaiian Superman show up and you all Lokelani Lane wit him."

"You're kidding right?" Chloe shook her head. "This isn't about that."

"I look like one joker to you?" Kāʻeo replied.

"I never took you for a child either, but here you are acting like one."

Kāʻeo dropped the crayfish and watched it skitter away. "You like go play pretend wit Kaʻi, go ahead, I not going be dea fo watch dat fuckah ack. I wen see enuff of dat from him already. I get actual work fo do, or maybe you no think so anymore," his jealousy gave way to pettiness.

"I think you're overreacting," she said. "I think it would be good for all three of us, just like before: friends working together."

The term stung. "I wish you was honest wit me from da start, you know?" He brought a hand to the water and let it calm him, "…about your feelings fo him."

She put a hand on his shoulder, "This is not about that," she paused. "And I never—"

"No fucking touch me," he shrugged her off.

"He asked me to help and I want to," she looked straight at him. "What we're doing here, it's good, but there's more work to be done."

"You no need fo tell me dat, keh? I know all dat already," he stood up and dusted off his shorts. "But Ka'i? Nah, he no understand da kine shit we doing up hea or da kine shit dey stay doing downtown. He understand what dat shit means but he no understand da meaning, you know? One guy like him, he not like us, he never have to work fo his kuleana."

"You don't know him," Chloe spat out. "Not like I do."

"You right," Kā'eo agreed. "But I know me, keh? And I know what I need fo do, so no tell me shit," Kā'eo snapped. "I wen have enough people in my life trying fo do dat," Kā'eo added, starting back up the trail.

Chloe climbed up after him. "This is bigger than the three of us," she tried to reason with him.

"You think so, ah?" Kā'eo shot back. "Den why now, ah? Why all of a sudden you give a shit?" She didn't even bother to answer. "I always wen think you was like me, you know? But you more like him, ah? Fo you, all dis stay jus fo da summer, but dis stay everything fo me right now."

She continued to push him. "This is about everything you talked about: your family and our culture, about fighting for all of that," she said, putting forward one last attempt.

"You right," Kā'eo conceded. "But fo be honest wit you, I no give a shit about dat right now, you understand? I jus like be hea, I jus like work, and if you no like stay den get da fuck out of hea, keh? I can take care dis place myself."

"Kāʻeo," she shook her head. "That's not—"

"No," he said before she could add anything further. "Dis stay my kuleana, not yours, I get dat, so you no need waste your time."

"You're not thinking straight right now," she replied. "You're going to realize that tomorrow."

"Tomorrow I going be hea," Kāʻeo said, crossing his arms. "Wea da fuck you going be?"

"You don't know what you're talking about," she threw back at him. "But that's fine, good luck," she told him and went, leaving the ʻawa patch and Kāʻeo behind her.

After that day, Kāʻeo saw less and less of Chloe. She came by to collect her things from the cottage, her books and her weaving material, and to finish up work that she had already started, leaving just as he got there or arriving when he was on the way out, until finally her things were gone and her work was done. No can be angry, he would tell himself, but still he was frustrated that he had let his own jealousy and pettiness get the better of him that day.

Although it hurt Kāʻeo not to see her, he began to spend all of his free time there, pouring himself into his tasks, determined to keep the crops thriving. Even when the semester got into full swing, he would attend class in the morning and spend his afternoons and much of his evenings at the cottage. After he discovered a group of pigs rooting through the area, he bought a twin-size mattress from Goodwill and started sleeping there overnight. Dis needs fo be done, he told himself, not willing to admit how obsessed he had become. Not willing to admit that the job was too much for one person to handle. That as hard as he was working, even the ʻawa was showing signs of decline, several of the older plants spotted black and stricken with lesions.

With Kāʻeo spending more and more of his time away from home, Pops and Ma became more and more concerned with what he was doing. In the beginning, they just wanted to know more about the opportunity:

"What're you doing up there?"

"Your professor stay okay wit dis?"

"How much does it pay?"

And initially, they were fine with it:

"As long as this is something that you want to do."

"Good you stay learning something."

"Don't forget to save some of it in the bank."

But eventually, as they saw less and less of their son, their concern grew:

"Dis how you really like spend your time?"

"Does your professor know?"

"Das lawehala, you know dat kine, one poison fo da soul."

"Jus stay out of my business, keh?" he finally told his mother one morning, tired of having to deal with questions that he didn't have time for and that they wouldn't understand the answers to. "You guys get no idea, alright."

Ma was in the living room, watching the morning news. "Why you doing dis fo anyway?" she asked him for the third time that week. "You no get papers fo write or something? Finals fo study fo? Or what, you stay behind now? I knew dis was going happen. What, you think your faddah and me wen buss our ass fo you—"

The newscaster was rambling on, an image of a construction site behind him, "…with the discovery, protests have escalated."

"Jus stop okay," Kāʻeo told her, trying to listen. "I know what da fuck I doing, alright?"

"See, and you say dat stuff not messing wit your head," Ma nodded. "Stay all in your blood already, acking all li'dis, and dis not da first time either."

"I acking li'dis cuz of you guys, cuz you guys no can jus let me be already," Kāʻeo clarified. "Jus cuz I stay doing something dat you no understand, no mean I stay doing something wrong."

"We jus worried about you," she said.

"Worry about yourself," Kāʻeo slammed the screen door closed.

He decided to skip class that day. His professors had review sessions planned, and he really didn't feel like playing fill-in-the-blank or extra-credit *Jeopardy*, so he decided to head up to the cottage instead. Rather than beginning work on his next project, clearing a section of forest to increase space between the ʻawa plants in the hopes of better managing the crop, Kāʻeo decided to take the afternoon for himself. He needed it. His insecurity over the crop's decline was affecting his resolve. And after his fight with Chloe, he had begun to question whether or not what he was doing was as significant as he had originally thought. He prepared enough ʻawa for two people, emptying the ground root into a large thermos that he had brought with him, and headed for the river.

Rather than climb up into the mountain, Kāʻeo decided to follow the water down, leaving the cottage behind. He walked along the riverbank, sometimes crossing over the rusted remnants of the barbed wire fence that ran adjacent to the river, separating public from private land, and picking guava or mountain apple, washing them down with a large draw from his bottle. As the river widened, Kāʻeo gave up dry land and waded through the river with no idea of where it would lead. The further he went, the more at ease he felt, his anxiety sinking, the smell of the ʻaʻaliʻi, and the warmth of the ʻawa, carrying his mind away. And then suddenly, Kāʻeo could taste salt on his lips and he could smell the ocean breeze even though he was miles from the beach. Everywhere he looked there was water. How da hell I wen get hea? he thought.

In the distance, he saw an approaching fleet of canoes, ʻau waʻa kaulua, carrying men and women, pūʻali. The number seemed endless. Their faces tattooed and fierce, their bodies, honed and muscular, their strokes filling the sky with hekili, with thunder. Kāʻeo tried his best to swim after them, grabbing hold of one of the waʻa. "Kūʻē," the men shouted over the rising crests. "Kūʻē," the men said again, but Kāʻeo was too out of breath to join them. The men stopped paddling and one of them, a tall figure covered in kākau, approached Kāʻeo.

But the figure was not made of flesh; rather, he was a tangle of roots, of kalo, thick and knotted. The figure towered over Kāʻeo. "ʻO wai kou inoa?" the figure asked as if speaking to a child, his words weakening Kāʻeo's grip. "ʻO wai kou inoa?" his voice echoed across the water. Kāʻeo heard the question over and over again in his head. The words, a mele, and the voices, a chant, booming in unison, rising, and rising across the horizon.

"ʻO wai kou inoa?" *What is your name?*

Kāʻeo's fingers slipped loose and he fell back. The waves crashed over him. The current pulled him back and down. And beneath the surface, he felt as he had above it, empty, without purpose, alone.

Kāʻeo woke suddenly on the riverbank, his head just above water. It was evening, the land completely blanketed in darkness. He sat up and tried to compose himself. ʻawa had never once caused him to hallucinate and he wondered if he had experienced a hihiʻo, a vision. "ʻO wai kou inoa?" He knew the implications of the question. It was about his name, it was about his genealogy, where he came from, who he was. He could feel his anxiety over the ʻawa returning, and he felt like he was seventeen again, confused. He looked down at his hands. He was still shaking.

When he got to his truck, he tried to call Chloe, knowing that she was the only one he could share the vision with. After six rings, it went to voice mail. He tried again with the same result. He threw the phone in the passenger seat and rested his head on the steering wheel. Then he remembered the news that morning: ...*with protestors planning a large demonstration in Kakaʻako tonight.*

Kāʻeo arrived to a crowd of hundreds lined up along Ward Avenue and Ala Moana Boulevard. As he navigated the crowd, he could feel their energy rattling the tourists that passed. He watched the traffic building up, the cars stopping when a flood of protestors entered the crosswalk to brandish the messages scrawled across their signs: *Our Ancestors, Our Rights*; *Mālama our Iwi Kūpuna*; *Rest in (Temporary) Peace*. The cries of the crowd rose above the noise of the city, their voices united in protest. Kāʻeo was overwhelmed by the strength of their resolve. Hearing about it was one thing, seeing it and being there was quite another, and it made Kāʻeo think again about what Chloe had told him, about how important what was going on down there really was. Through the mass, Kāʻeo recognized one of the faces. Alakaʻi was standing at the front, his bare chest freshly adorned with a list of names in black paint. Kāʻeo closed his shaking hand into a fist.

He hurtled forward until he got to Alakaʻi's post. "Wea Chloe stay?" he shouted, grabbing Alakaʻi's arm. "I need fo talk wit her."

Alakaʻi pulled his arm back, ignoring Kāʻeo's aggression. "If you want to join us, there's signs over there," he yelled over the crowd, putting a hand on his friend's shoulder. "If you want to make your own, there's a table across the street," he pointed toward one of the many stations that lined the road.

"Chloe?" Kāʻeo shouted again, growing irritated with Alakaʻi. "Wea da fuck she stay?"

"Calm down," Alakaʻi tried to tell Kāʻeo over the noise of the crowd.

"No tell me what fo fucking do," he pushed Alakaʻi back. A few people began to notice Kāʻeo's aggression. "Get your fucking hands off me," he told them. "I stay looking fo my friend."

"I don't know where she is," Alakaʻi said.

"No fucking lie to me," Kāʻeo grabbed Alakaʻi's collar.

But Alakaʻi was not up for Kāʻeo's childishness. He pushed Kāʻeo back. Kāʻeo stumbled into a group behind him. "You either need to calm down or leave," he told Kāʻeo. The crowd was circling, clearing room for what they knew was about to happen.

"You always thought you was better than me, ah?" Kāʻeo pumped his shoulders. "Well I no give two shits about who your great-great-great-grandfaddah was or wea da fuck you wen grad."

"You're making a mistake, Kāʻeo."

"No fucking use my name, alright?"

"Ka—"

"What da fuck I told you?" Kāʻeo cocked his arm back, but a man from the crowd grabbed him before he could throw.

"Listen to him," the man told him.

"Fuck you," Kāʻeo elbowed himself free. Kāʻeo felt another hand grab his, and he readied his fist. "You deaf or what?" But when he turned to swing, it was Chloe he was facing.

"What are you doing?" she asked him. His adrenaline began to leave his veins, shame replacing it. He looked around and noticed the faces of those around him, faces like his own but all he saw was difference. They were determined and full of purpose. When they chanted, they did not stumble. When they raised their fists, they cracked the sky. Kāʻeo looked at Alakaʻi's chest and the names that were written across it, what Kāʻeo guessed were the names of Alakaʻi's family members that were buried there, with the black strokes branched out like roots. Kāʻeo thought about his own history, and he felt a sharp sense of discontent with himself.

"You need to leave," Alakaʻi told Kāʻeo. Kāʻeo looked past Alakaʻi, and noticed two police officers making their way through the crowd. "Now," Alakaʻi commanded Kāʻeo.

"I'm sorry," Chloe said to Kāʻeo, her tone lacking concern. "But he's right."

He didn't need her pity. "Fuck you," he told her, backing away. "Fuck you too," he lashed out at Alakaʻi, his pettiness surfacing again. "Fuck all you guys. You look at me like I stay crazy, like I dunno what da fuck I stay doing wit my life." Kāʻeo faced the crowd, turning around and around. "Like I no get one kuleana," he continued. "Like you stay better than me, but you not, you hear me? You not."

The crowd parted, the two officers readying their cuffs. "Everything's fine, officers," Alakaʻi told them. They looked at the man that Kāʻeo had elbowed. The man nodded in the affirmative. "Our friend, he was just leaving," Alakaʻi looked at Kāʻeo, waiting for his compliance.

"I going," Kāʻeo retreated. "I no need fuckahs like you fo help me figgah my shit out. I get real work fo do."

Alakaʻi gave Kāʻeo the same look that Chloe had given to him a moment before. "And what's that?" Alakaʻi said to him, his tone showing more concern than aggression, but Kāʻeo didn't have an answer. "What do you stand for?" Alakai shouted. "Who are you?" Alakaʻi spread his arms wide, the chants of the crowd rising. "Who the fuck are you?"

The question haunted Kāʻeo on the drive home, unable to put it or the vision out of his mind. Both prompted him to ask questions of himself that he hadn't asked since he was in high school, and yet he couldn't help but feel at a loss for the answers that he had been working toward over the last three years. He drove for a while, not paying attention to the streets or the world around him, not realizing that he had driven home until he was already there. It was late and he was surprised to see the living room lights on and Tūtūpapa's station wagon in the driveway. He walked into the house and his grandfather and his parents were sitting in the dining room, waiting for him. "What da hell stay going on now?" he asked them, clearly exhausted, ready to put the day to bed.

Ma looked him up and down. "You was dea all day again, ah?"

Kāʻeo caught a glimpse of himself in the picture window. His clothes were filthy, and his face and arms were covered in dried dirt. He realized how crazy he must have looked to them. "Nah," Kāʻeo replied. "I wen go downtown. Had fo deal wit some things."

"Don't lie to us," Pops said.

"What da fuck is dis?" Kāʻeo laughed. "You guys on me these past couple weeks, den Ma dis morning, and what da fuck Tūtūpapa stay doing hea?"

"We want to talk, that's all," Pops said.

"Sit," Ma told him. But Kāʻeo refused.

"I going shower," he told them. "I no get time fo do dis tonight."

Tūtūpapa looked at Kāʻeo, the red around his grandson's eyes and the yellowish tinge just beginning to blossom on the tops of his cheeks. "Dis dangerous stuff, Kāʻeo," Tūtūpapa warned, staring hard at his grandson.

"What?" Kāʻeo was confused, not sure what his grandfather was talking about.

"ʻAwa," Ma clarified.

"Das what dis stay about?" Kāʻeo laughed again. "You guys no stay tired of giving me bullshit, or what?"

Tūtūpapa pulled himself to the edge of his seat. "You keep doing um, you going end up all da kine up hea, I know guys li'dat," he tapped his forehead. "Jus like alcohol, dat kine." Kāʻeo looked at Tūtūpapa. He could see fatigue weighing heavy on his grandfather's cheeks, his skin loose and shadowed. "I been through plenny, Kāʻeo, you know dat. I dunno what stay going on wit you, but ʻawa not da answer, you understand?"

"You ever tried um?" Kāʻeo asked Tūtūpapa, knowing that there was no way that he had.

"No need," Tūtūpapa replied with conviction.

"Das what I thought," Kāʻeo nodded.

"Stay one reason 'awa was da kine long time ago. 'awa stay one sacrilege to da body, Kāʻeo," Tūtūpapa's stare was solid, steady. "How much you wen poison yourself already?"

Kāʻeo didn't need to ask if his grandfather was serious. He knew the history of 'awa and the history of Tūtūpapa's beliefs. "All you guys, I trying fo explore my," he laughed, "*our* fucking culture, and you guys thinking I jus fucking around up dea, getting fucking wasted or something."

"We jus trying fo look out fo you, Kāʻeo," Ma explained. "We jus trying fo make sure you not doing da wrong things."

"And you guys think you know?" Kāʻeo shook his head. "You guys dunno nutten, das da problem. You guys all da kine," he struggled with the words, wanting more than anything to rattle off a lecture on the cultural oppression of Hawaiians, but what was the point.

"You stay listening to yourself right now, you think we deserve dis level of disrespect?" Ma asked.

Tūtūpapa was studying Kāʻeo's face. He knew what this was really about. "What, you think dis make you more Hawaiian or something? You think dis makes you better than your maddah and me?"

"Das not what I…" Kāʻeo shook his head.

"What den, huh?" Tūtūpapa asked. "We never raise you fo behave li'dis."

"Das da problem," Kāʻeo shot back, his frustrations from earlier that night cresting. "You wen raise me fo behave like one haole, you wen raise me fo behave like *you*."

"Kāʻeo," Ma shot up.

"You like ack haole, call me Robert den, keh? No use my fucking name," Kāʻeo's emotions were doing the thinking for him. "You guys sit hea and ack like I stay doing something wrong, wen I jus trying fo make up fo da shit you guys never wen teach me."

"No ack," Tūtūpapa pounded the table with his fist. "We wen teach you da importance of respecting yourself, we wen teach you da importance of respecting your family."

"What about teaching us da importance of being Hawaiian, huh?" Kāʻeo stared through his grandfather and saw his granduncle in the reflection of the picture window. "What about teaching us da moʻolelo of our culture? Da real histories, not da shit you wen make up or da kine about your friend, Paul Who-gives-one-fuck."

"Eh, maybe I dunno da kine you talking about. I never learn dat kine, keh? But I know what I know, you understand?" Tūtūpapa sat down, waving his grandson's accusations away. "And you like disrespect dis family, you like ack li'dis, den—"

"You da ones like bring dis up, right?" Kāʻeo interrupted. "Jus like wen I told you guys I was going get my degree in Hawaiian Studies, you guys had fo ack all da kine, like what da fuck I doing wit one degree li'dat."

"That's not—" Pops attempted to set the record straight. "We told you that we were proud that you got the scholarship, and that we were proud of the work that you had done."

"Den Ma wen ask me what kine job I going get, and Papa wen ack like he never even know dat dey get one degree in Hawaiian Studies. Same shit, jus like tonight. Jus like always." Kāʻeo shook his head, the realization coming over him, his past churning up to meet his present. "No wonder I stay feeling like one fucking loser compared to my classmates. No wonder I da one always struggling wit shit."

"Dey really doing one number on you up dea, ah?" Tūtūpapa had to add. "Get more than ʻawa messing wit your head right now, I tell you."

"Das right, go ahead," Kāʻeo replied, not caring about what they thought anymore. "Ack like you fucking know, but you dunno shit about what I doing, about having one kuleana, about having one sense of responsibility to *our* culture, to *our* people, to *our* land. You like get wasted and forget about everything, go ahead, but das not me, keh?"

"Enough," Tūtūpapa jumped out of his seat. "Enough," he slammed his fist on the table. "You think you know better, huh? Den go already," Tūtūpapa told Kāʻeo. "I not going sit hea and defend," Tūtūpapa licked his lips, his voice hoarse. "I not going sit hea and talk about shit you dunno nutten about. I wen make my peace wit my life, wit my choices, you understand?"

"Das good," Kāʻeo nodded. "No need worry about me den, keh? Everything make sense. Now I know why I stay so fucked up," he said. "Now I know why I stay li'dis, all da kine up hea," he tapped his forehead. "Now I know why I no can take care da ʻawa myself."

"Pūpūkahi i holomua," Tūtūpapa pounded his fist in rhythm with the words. "Remember what I wen tell you long time ago?" his grandfather urged him. "Pūpūkahi i holomua," he said again. "You remember dat, Kāʻeo?"

"Fuck you," Kāʻeo said calmly to his grandfather, dismissing Tūtūpapa's sudden use of the proverb and leaving the kitchen. "Fuck all you guys already."

"Kāʻeo," his mother pleaded, but her son was already out the door.

"No fucking boddah me, keh?" he told her. "I no get time fo deal wit your guys' bullshit anymore." And then he left, jumping in his car and leaving a trail of rubber streaked across the road.

Kāʻeo didn't have to think about where he was going next. His sense of direction was second nature by now, habitual. When he got there, he moved with determination. He stormed through the back gate and then along the trail that led to the cottage. When he got there, he went around the back to the ʻawa patch, where four healthy ʻawa plants stood tall. He grabbed the tallest of them and pulled it from the earth, its roots holding as long as they could. And then he pulled out the next one, and then the next one, and then the next one until every last plant had been dug up and defiled. After that, he carried the older roots into the cottage, leaving the younger ones in a trail of dirt behind him, their corpses exposed.

Inside, he dropped the carcasses on the table and began to separate the roots from the stalk, using only his hands. When he had separated all of them, he grabbed a knife from another table and cut the roots into chunks, then put a handful of pieces into his mouth, binging on the bitter juices before spitting the used ones out on the floor and indulging himself again, and again, and again. It didn't take long for the numbness to run through his limbs, to drown out the humming inside his head, the waves calling to him.

Kāʻeo fought them back, throwing his fist against the wall, thinking about himself and his grandfather, how alike the two of them really were. He threw his fist a second time, thinking about all the time that he had spent with Chloe, the work that they had done together, and how it still wasn't enough. Three more times, in his mind, aiming for the image of Alakaʻi standing on the corner, one with the crowd, while Kāʻeo still struggled to find his place. The wood gave at the center, the soft planks eaten from the inside. He shook the splinters loose and looked down at his hand, his vision blurring.

ʻo wai kou inoa? He heard the question echo in his mind. *What do you stand for? Who are you?* "ʻO Robert Kāʻeo Teixeira koʻu inoa," he replied aloud, his voice cracking. "ʻO Robert Teixeira koʻu inoa," he declared, no one else around to hear him but himself. "ʻO Kāʻeo Teixeira koʻu inoa," he began to plead over the silence. *Who the fuck are you?* "Moʻopuna kāne of…" but before he could even begin his genealogy, he fell to his knees and the waves took him again.

It was a Saturday, two days after Kāʻeo had fought with his family. Mark was at work and Kāʻeo's parents had left for their weekly errands, Sam's Club and Walmart. Kāʻeo wasn't sure where Elani was, but he figured his brother would either be too wrapped up in a book or too consumed with his own writing to even realize that Kāʻeo was there. He was half right. Although he had gotten into the house and into his room with little notice, by the time he had finished packing what he needed, his clothes and a small selection of books, he heard the door across the hall open.

Although they were five years apart, Kāʻeo always saw a part of himself in his youngest brother. Elani was deeply interested in knowledge, although his tastes were geared toward the fantastical, his favorite books falling under genres of young adult fiction and sci-fi. And he was a thinker, his mind always elsewhere. But Kāʻeo knew that it was also these traits that separated his brother from the rest of the world. He was an introvert, lost in his imagination, and that was difficult for others to understand.

"What're you doing?" he finally asked Kāʻeo. "Why are you doing this?"

"Cuz I need fo leave," Kāʻeo told him. "Cuz I no get one choice."

"Why not?"

"Cuz das how things stay," Kāʻeo stood up and grabbed his backpack and his bag of clothes. "Sometimes you need fo choose fo yourself, sometimes you need fo jus go your own way and figgah things out."

"Otherwise what?" Elani continued, still not understanding his brother's decision, and Kāʻeo knew why. When Kāʻeo was his brother's age, he had already spent much of his high school life on the fringes, too smart for his own good, dislocated and disinterested. But Elani had always excelled in school, what he lacked in social intelligence he more than made up for in his aptitude and interest in the lessons that he was taught.

Kāʻeo pulled his brother close and thought of how best to express his disconnect. "O ka makapō wale no ka mea hāpapa i ka pōuli." It came to his lips with little effort, a proverb that he had heard many times before but that he hadn't understood until then.

When he saw his brother's face, he repeated it again, slower this time, making sure that his brother heard every word even if he knew that Elani did not understand what it meant. "You need fo take da time fo figgah your shit out or you not going nowea," Kāʻeo translated for his brother.

Elani looked at him with an empty stare. "What are you—" he began. "I still don't get it."

"You will," Kāʻeo let him go. "One day you going ask yourself wea you going and you going know why I stay doing dis," he said. "Den you going know our truth fo yourself," he added, then he picked up his bag and headed for the door.

Later that day, Ma called to voice her concern and to try to convince Kāʻeo to come home. "You not thinking straight," she said. "Wea you going live? How you going take care of yourself?"

"No worry about me," Kāʻeo dismissed her concern, he wasn't a child anymore.

Kāʻeo needed a place to stay and he needed work, and he knew that he wasn't going to get one without the other. He thought about talking to Dr. Kauhane, to ask if she knew of any positions where he could put his knowledge to use, perhaps a job with her friend in Waimānalo, but he also knew the state he had left the cottage in. He could explain what had happened, and he imagined that she would understand, but he didn't need her sympathy, and to be honest, he had never developed the same relationship with her that Chloe had. Even though they had been close, she was always kumu to Chloe and Dr. Kauhane to him.

"I talked to my friend," Pops tried to reason with Kāʻeo over the phone. "He can get you a part-time position at the roofing company he works for, mostly weekends."

But Kāʻeo didn't want anyone's help.

He ended up at one of the first jobs he applied for, Kingdom Movers. They had immediate openings and the job paid well enough. "You looking fo something permanent or temporary?" the owner asked Kāʻeo, looking at his application. Even with his lack of experience, his qualifications exceeded the minimum requirements of a strong back.

"Temporary," Kāʻeo told him, "until I find something better. I jus like work fo now, whatever you get stay good."

"What about your sku?"

"No worry about dat," Kāʻeo reassured him, he would figure it out.

And in the beginning he tried to juggle the two, rearranging his schedule and limiting his hours at work. But eventually one had to give. So, he took on more hours during the week and dropped his classes altogether, promising himself that he'd make up the missed credits in the fall.

While he saved up enough money for rent, he slept in the parking lot behind the shop on Sand Island. Every morning he woke up early, cleaned up in the bathroom, and then changed before anyone else arrived. He kept what he could in his locker or in his truck, hand-washing his work shirts and jeans in the basin and drying them at the laundromat down the road.

He slept three hours at most, and spent the rest of his nights wandering downtown. When he was a kid, his parents would always keep to Nimitz Highway, avoiding Chinatown altogether. "There's nothing for us there," they had told him. Between the shops and alleyways, he saw why they had sheltered him: tents, shopping carts, wooden-pallet forts, and metal cages. The incense that floated out from the medicine shops mixed with the stench of urine and rotting fruit. He counted the frequency of offers to remedy his insomnia. The number of times that he was pitched pills, powder, or crystal, but he always lost count by the time he reached River Street, his attention on the gathering skeletons. He knew how they had gotten there and who was responsible for their plight, Marxism more than theory now.

Once, he wandered out to 'A'ala Park, a lowland marsh filled and forgotten, so named because of the fragrant smell of detergent perfuming the air. The history was shallow here, the baseball diamonds barely a century old, but Kā'eo knew more about Benjamin Dillingham and the train station that was built there than he did about the mo'olelo of that place. With the lights out for the night, Kā'eo could count the casualties, the bodies of those who were houseless. He could imagine the O'ahu Railway rolling in, carrying with it prosperity and sugar, but also poverty and disempowerment.

Kā'eo's phone rang, the tone as shrill as a train whistle in the night, Tūtūpapa's name displayed on the screen. Kā'eo answered and waited for his grandfather to speak, but all he could hear was his grandfather breathing on the other end. "What, you get something fo fucking say to me?" he asked him, but Tūtūpapa didn't respond. Kā'eo hung up the phone and turned it off, making a note to disconnect his service the next day. Fuck them, he thought. He was doing just fine on his own.

One thing that Kā'eo had learned in high school was that Hawai'i is a paradox, one of the smallest states and yet one of the densest. For him, that meant that although your chances of running into someone you knew was likely, your chances of never running into them at all was just as likely—you just had to know how to disappear. And in Kahalu'u, it was only a matter of moving over to the other side of the Ko'olau Mountains for you to become a ghost.

He enjoyed the independence, the freedom, living month to month out of a small studio a few blocks from his job downtown. He had become a celebrity at the farmers' market, haggling for vegetables and fruits, entertaining with conversation in exchange for the best prices on the merchants' offerings. He even shared a plot of land with one of the residents in Nu'uanu, where he had started to grow 'aloe for his dry feet, laukahi to treat his muscles, and 'uhaloa to help when he got sick.

On his days off, he took to educating himself. When he exhausted his own collection, he began to visit Hamilton Library, camping between the stacks and immersing himself in the knowledge of Kamakau, Malo, and Pukui. Manaʻo from Kameʻeleihiwa, Silva, and Trask. But as time passed, his frustrations began to fester again and he could feel himself growing restless: what had he really accomplished so far? What had he really done?

Move after move, he would try to talk sense into his coworkers, anxious to discuss appropriation while they handled fragile imports, colonialism while they set up koa bedframes, anything to get his mind working again. The crew usually humored him, polite nods and grunts, silencing him when it came time to run the lunch order. Fast food and plate lunches. Starches, fats, and refined sugars. Processed meats, preservatives, and MSG. "Dey take your culture, dey take your land, and den dey take your stomach," he remarked to them while he ate the poi that he had bought from the supermarket with his fingers, licking the inside of the cellophane bag with hungry tongue.

"You get plenny theories," one of his coworkers had told him on the way back from a delivery in Hawaiʻi Kai. They had stopped to eat, his coworker spreading a puddle of congealed gravy across his white rice. "But what you going do, you going march down da capitol? You going protest down da military base?" his coworker laughed. "You going strap one bomb to your chest and play terrorist?"

Kāʻeo knew that his coworker was right, what was theory without action, action without theory? He had questioned Alakaʻi's motives not that long ago, but his time apart had been one of reflection, and he now knew that Alakaʻi had been more than just talk.

Whereas Kāʻeo had acted selfishly, envious of his friend's newfound purpose and upbringing and jealous of the commonalities that Alakaʻi and Chloe had shared. He missed the earth between his fingers and the sweat dripping off his forehead to meet it. He missed Chloe, her insight and their conversations, the way that she would take his hands without judgment and teach him what she had learned. He even missed Alakaʻi: his politics and his resolve. He longed for that connection again, the purpose behind the act.

"We should go," Kāʻeo said to his coworker, watching the scatter of rental cars and shuttles moving in and out of the parking lot. "I told you I never like come hea."

"Jus let me finish my food, alright?"

A tour group herded past, dusting Kāʻeo's forehead. "Diamond Head," the guide proclaimed with authority, reciting his company script, "was so named because, when British sailors arrived here, they mistakenly thought that the volcanic crystals on the beach were diamonds." Lēʻahi, Kāʻeo thought, recalling the moʻolelo of Pele and Hiʻiaka: how Hiʻiaka had seen the brow of an ahi in the crater's shape, giving the place its name.

Dis sacred land, Kāʻeo thought, feeling his heart in his ears, watching the group move toward the trail, imagining in their place the aliʻi preparing to hōlua down the slopes. One of the tourists dumped his cigarette in his Coke can and dropped it to the dirt, kicking it off the path. By the time his coworker had looked up from his Styrofoam container, Kāʻeo had carved his way across the asphalt and was shouting obscenities at everyone in earshot, clutching the tourist's collar.

"Pick dat shit up," he yelled, throwing the man toward the glimmering aluminum. "Now," Kāʻeo watched the tourist scamper through the grass.

"Who do you think you are?" Another tourist in a souvenir T-shirt and Bermuda shorts intervened, sprinkling Kāʻeo's cheeks with pearls of saliva.

Kāʻeo walked toward the tourist, his chest meeting the man's moustache. "Eh haole," Kāʻeo said, looking down at him, "who da fuck you think *you* are, ah? Wea da fuck you think *you* stay?"

"Excuse me?" the man pushed Kāʻeo back, taking off his veteran's cap and handing it to his wife. "Twenty years…twenty years, I fought——"

"Not fo me," Kāʻeo cocked back, but his coworker caught him at the wrist before Kāʻeo could swing and pulled him away before things could get worse.

"You fucking crazy, or what?" he asked Kāʻeo.

No, Kāʻeo realized, his mind was perfectly clear.

The next day, Kāʻeo's boss let him go. His co-worker had told him what had happened and many of the crew agreed that Kāʻeo's temperament was making it difficult for any of them to work with him. "No need dis fucking job, anyway," he told him. "I get better things fo do wit my life." And yet, three months after moving out of his parents' house, he found himself in the same position he had been in when he had left. He sat on his tailgate at Ala Moana Beach Park, looking out at the debris drifting in the tide, trying to think of his next move. He had some savings at least and his rent for the month had been paid. Worse comes to worst, he could stomach moving back home until he found something better than stable. Something flexible, so he could enroll in the summer session, go full-time in the fall, and finish by the spring.

A familiar voice interrupted his thoughts. "Look at dis, da pride of Kahaluʻu in da flesh, what da fuck you doing in town? You into dat high makamaka pussy now or what?"

Kāʻeo had known Junior since small kid time, from King Intermediate to Castle High, although Kāʻeo hadn't seen Junior since he left for Damien before their senior year. "Not since your maddah," Kāʻeo replied, standing up to shake Junior's hand and then Junior's friends'.

"You better watch out, ʻeo, you know your maddah stay da one who wen give me da eye outside da principal's office dat one time."

"I going give you one eye pretty soon," Kāʻeo held up his fist and cracked Junior's shoulder.

"Long time, man," Junior reminisced. "Last I heard you was one college boy, now what, you working da slave ship enterprise?" Junior asked, slapping the logo on Kāʻeo's chest.

"Nah, stay taking one break right now. We all no can be banging our faddah's hand-me-downs," Kāʻeo replied, giving Junior's rope chain a nod.

Junior laughed, reaching behind his ear for a cigarette. "Well shit, you like come cruise wit us or what? We get beer, pūpū, couple chicks coming fo meet us."

"Nah," Kāʻeo shook his head. "I get some things fo take care of."

"One busy body, huh? What about tonight, working man, you get anything on da books?"

"I get couple hours free," Kāʻeo joked, recent events leaving his schedule wide open.

"I tell you what, 'eo," Junior blew a plume into the sky. "I throwing one small get-together at my place, come cruise, have couple beers or whatever, catch up."

"Maybe," Kāʻeo replied, unsure. Although a trip out to Kahaluʻu would give him a chance to take his mind off things, it meant the possibility of running into his parents and he wasn't ready for that yet.

"Maybe?" Junior persisted, knowing it wouldn't take much.

"Only can stay little while though, keh?" Kāʻeo gave in, figuring he could worry about the logistics later. He could use a chance to unwind. "You up at the same place?"

"Nah," Junior said. "Living at my aunty's house right now, wit my faddah." Junior gave Kāʻeo the directions to his house. "Jus give me one call wen you close."

"No phone," Kāʻeo smiled proudly, he had no need for one.

"Shit, you really stay in dat plantation era, yah?"

"No worries, can find um," Kāʻeo told him. "I going see you tonight." They sealed the deal with a round of handshakes, and then Kāʻeo watched Junior and his friends disappear down the beach. He had no idea what to expect that night, but at that moment, he was okay with that.

Before he went to Junior's, he stopped at Safeway to pick up a case of Coors. His choice was strategic, knowing full well that even though Safeway was centrally located in Kāneʻohe town, his family was more than likely to visit the more expensive but local Times than make the additional fifteen minute trek up Kahekili. But unfortunately his paradox theory had already proven him wrong once that day, and he did not account for the frugal nature of family friends. He had almost made it out of the store when he saw his neighbor, Aunty Sheryl, barreling toward him. "Robert Kāʻeo Teixeira," she grabbed his face and kissed his cheeks. "Where have you been?"

"I wen move to town, Aunty, Ma never wen say nutten to you?" he tried to act nonchalant. Aunty Sheryl was one of his mother's closest friends, but he wasn't sure how much his mother had told her.

"She said she didn't know," Aunty Sheryl called his bluff. "Town, huh, closer to school?"

"Yah, yah," he lied, eyeing the door.

She looked down at his purchase. "I hope you're going to at least stop by and see your mother, with everything that's going on with your grandfather," she pursed her lips. "I know it would just make her so happy to see you."

He hesitated, not sure what she was talking about. "Things going be fine," he replied, sure it was nothing.

"Go home," Aunty Sheryl told him. "Talk to your mother," she added, kissing his cheek and leaving him to worry.

Kā'eo didn't waste any time. He used the payphone outside. He called twice, and twice he got his parents' answering machine. He slipped the last of his change in the slot and called Junior. "I no think I going come over tonight."

"Why not?"

"I jus no feel like going right now, get some things going on, das all."

"I tell you what," Junior pitched. "Jus come swing by couple minutes. Take your mind off whatever."

Kā'eo considered the offer, realizing the benefit. He would swing by his parents' house, but if they weren't there, it would at least give him a chance to check in again afterward. "Yah, all right," he conceded.

"Now hurry da fuck up," Junior told him. "Da beer getting warm already."

Junior lived up a private road, a dirt and gravel stretch leading up to a chain link gate that was locked at all times—his father's rule, not his. A *No Trespassing* sign was the only way that Kā'eo knew that there was anything back there but overgrowth, and he had to drive around twice before he saw it. Junior stepped out of the darkness, waving him in by cell phone light.

Kā'eo heard the music before he saw the line of cars, but when he did, he immediately felt the urge to turn around. In his side mirror, he could see the gate closing behind him and Junior hustling up the side. The fence lined the driveway and met the house at the garage, sectioning off most of the yard behind a barricade of woven steel. Kā'eo pulled onto the grass and got out, three pits barreling toward the gate.

Junior shook the fence a few times. "No mind these pussies," he told Kāʻeo, laughing as the dogs scampered away. "Come." He led Kāʻeo away from the fence and to a set of wooden steps from the garage to the second floor. "I get da whole house to myself right now," Junior told him.

There were more bodies than Kāʻeo could count. Most of the faces looked familiar, people they had gone to high school with, younger siblings, and some he didn't recognize. He was expecting something more pedestrian. He was hoping for it, but this was Junior he was dealing with. He should have known better. Kāʻeo opened a beer and walked to the back window, the lānai concealed beneath a tin roof that ran the length of the first floor.

"Your faddah stay cool wit all of dis?" Kāʻeo asked.

"Stay on Maui fo da weekend." Junior nudged his side, "but no worry about all of dat, ʻeo. Relax, enjoy yourself."

Kāʻeo went through two more beers before he decided he was done and went outside. It had been a while since he had gotten drunk and he was already starting to feel it. His mind was still on his grandfather. He walked down to the garage and to the entrance to the back. What da fuck stay going on wit him? Kāʻeo thought. Tūtūpapa was healthy, he was strong. Then it hit him, how tired his grandfather had looked and how hollow in the cheeks he was. More fencing, wood this time, no latch. Kāʻeo couldn't shake the thought, the last argument that they had had, the things that he had said to him. His grandfather's phone call, what had Tūtūpapa called to tell him? "Fuck," he yelled, his guilt getting the better of him. "Fuck, fuck, fuck," punching his fist numb.

"Try watch out," Junior said from the top of the stairs, cigarette in one hand, beer in the other. "My faddah going be pissed you break his shit."

"Sorry, ah?" Kāʻeo wiped his face with his shirt, looking at the thick planks and heavy nails. "Stay small kine mental right now."

"You like some water or something?"

"Nah, I jus need fo cool down."

"You like me grab one chick fo polish your dick?" Junior joked, letting out a thick cloud.

Kāʻeo dropped his head and laughed. "You one real da kine, you know dat? One real misogynist."

"Eh, I jus trying fo help, ah?" The cherry flared across Junior's cheeks. "I get something though," he said, sliding down the steps. "Not going cool you down, but guarantee going clear your head real fast."

Kāʻeo followed him behind the garage and out across the grass. Junior reached in his pocket and two headlights flashed in the distance, Junior's Civic glowing like a lantern. When they were both in the cab, Junior reached for the glove box and popped it open, feeling along the inner edge until he found what he was looking for. Junior offered Kāʻeo the plastic bag as if it were anything but what it was. Kāʻeo took it, examining the off-white crystals in the yellow light.

"You fucking kidding me or what?" Kāʻeo laughed and handed the baggie back. "You like one high sku PSA or something: *Fuckahs fo Avoid*."

Junior took another drag from his cigarette. "Shit stay pure," Junior remarked. "Good stuff, ʻeo."

"You fuck wit dat shit?"

"Couple times," Junior said, Kāʻeo trying hard to detect his truth through the smoke. "My first semester at Mānoa, finals' week. Not in one while though."

"Shit, I never knew you was one academic," Kāʻeo joked, adding an additional emphasis on the "ack."

"Nah, I stay one businessman now, you know? One entrepreneur," Junior noted. "I no like waste my time wit all dat ivory tower bullshit. What we really need one degree fo anyway, fo work down da Sheraton? Or buss ass six months fo spend anada six on unemployment, and den buss ass again. Anything dey get fo teach me, can learn on my own, ah? Stay better dat way anyway."

"Not everything," Kāʻeo replied, thinking back on the lectures that he had attended and the books that he had read.

"You right," Junior admitted. "Da rest dey rob you fo or dey lock up behind one circulation desk. Das our right but dey ack like das one privilege."

"Can see dat," Kāʻeo agreed.

"And what dey really wen teach you, huh? Fo understand da politics of da koa desk you stay moving into one timeshare. What da hell you doing at one shit job li'dat anyway?" Junior asked him. "You get da brains and you know how fo use them, no tell me you jus trying fo understand da plight of da working man or some bullshit li'dat."

"Nah," Kāʻeo told him. "I jus trying fo get myself situated right now."

"You stay wasting your time, das what you doing." Junior put his cigarette down. "I mean shit, not like you fucking making one career fo yourself over dea, right?"

"What da fuck you know about dat?" Kāʻeo shot back.

"Nutten," Junior took another drag, disarming Kāʻeo's defensiveness. "Das da thing, dat kine mindset only fuck you up worse. Das how fuckahs end up thirty years at one job dey hate, happy cuz dey wen work their asses off fo one place dey no can afford, jus so dey can ma-ke and leave da house to da kids. But das how shit stay, yah?"

Kāʻeo laughed at Junior's truth. He looked at the second floor, watching the party through the picture window. "Dis one nice place, what kine job your aunty get and how long she going have fo buss her ass fo pay um off?"

"Da kine," Junior said, not bothering to specify. "My faddah help pay da mortgage."

"He still working construction?"

"Nah, got hurt couple years back, union bullshit. He was working under da table fo one while but dey never like spot da hospital bill. Now, you know, he gets by," he said, putting his cigarette out. "So what, you get lady issues or something? Or da grind jus getting to you?"

Kāʻeo looked down at the open glove box, at the baggie, and closed it before Junior could bring it up again. "Jus plenny stuffs right now, family shit, sku shit."

"Bullshit," Junior finished his thought. They both laughed.

"I no can believe you still driving dis piece of shit, you know dat," Kāʻeo said, playing with the sagging ceiling fabric. "You need one upgrade."

"Stay like old times, yah ʻeo?"

Kāʻeo nodded, remembering their junior year. They both had Mr. Haywood—first period for Kāʻeo, second for Junior—and there were some days when neither of them felt the need to attend. Instead, they cut school to cruise around in Junior's car: stopping at Mitsuken in the morning, then making their way through Waikīkī, and down to Makapuʻu to watch the college girls in their bikinis struggle with their tops. Kāʻeo looked at the carpet across the dashboard, ash stains and holes in the fabric, he could almost smell the sticky sweet from the all the times that they had chambered behind the school. He was sure that if he tucked his right hand down into the crack between the door and the passenger seat he'd find an old bottle that Junior had run out of Hygienics.

"You wen change, you know dat?" Kāʻeo told him. "Back den you never really give a shit about nutten."

"Was nutten fo give a shit about back den, right?"

"And now?" Kāʻeo threw the question out there.

"No Haolewood fo tell me what fo do," Junior laughed. "Nobody fo tell me what fo do."

Kāʻeo admired his confidence. He always had. "He's still there, you know dat?

Fuckah never going get fired unless he hit one kid or something."

"Stay pricks like him, you know?" Junior added. "Treat us like we lōlō, like we no get da smarts like dem. Fuck dat, you know, not like dat fuckah ever wen think we was going do more than land one State job anyway. I tell you, I stay tired of playing by da rules, of living li'dat. People like him ack like dey know better, like us Hawaiians never know how fo survive until da fucking haoles wen show up."

Kāʻeo knew that frustration, that rage. He turned to Junior, ready to share with him the manaʻo of the Hawaiian scholars that he had only begun to digest, but then he laughed: Junior was amping himself up in the reflection of the windshield, pumping his shoulders. "You fucking loaded or what?" Kāʻeo asked him, the moment lost.

"You know dat," Junior said, gripping the steering wheel with both hands.

"Calm down already," Kāʻeo replied, watching Junior, the car shaking. "You so fucking wired, feels like your fucking shocks going go already."

"Fuck you," Junior popped open the car door, letting the breeze in. "We go, you let me know if you change your mind, keh?"

"I'm good," Kāʻeo said, stepping back out into the night. "I might take you up on dat wahine though, get some solid chicks up dea."

"Need fo check da ID first," Junior winked, the headlights flashing the locks down.

"You one sick fuckah, you know dat?"

"Yah, yah," Junior replied as they walked back through the grass. "You let me know wen you ready fo quit hauling mattresses too, ah? You need fo find your way off da plantation sometime."

"I appreciate dat."

"And you ever need one place fo stay, anything," Junior looked back at his friend. "You jus let me know, yah?"

Kāʻeo followed Junior up the steps and back to the party, stopping outside the door. "I can use your phone?" he asked him. Junior handed it to him. Kāʻeo walked to the side and dialed his parents' house again. Still no answer. He tried to remember Mark's cell phone number, but he couldn't and only ended up receiving dial tones. Kāʻeo called his parents again and left a message with Junior's number, then handed the phone back. "You know what, I think I going cut out already."

"Stay early yet," Junior bargained with him. "Plus, I get one chick I like you meet first. She like guys like you, moody fuckahs."

"Fo real, I no trust any chicks you know dat well," Kāʻeo joked.

"Stay one good thing I jus met her den, ah?" he bargained, holding the door open for him.

"Half an hour," Kāʻeo told him.

"No worry, ʻeo," he flashed a smile. "You not going last dat long."

Kāʻeo woke up the next morning on the floor of Junior's spare bedroom with little recollection of the night before. He rolled off of the bed and stumbled out of the room. Junior was asleep on the living room floor, bottle in hand. Kāʻeo kicked his side. "Get up," he said, nudging Junior with his foot.

"What da fuck?" Junior mumbled, shielding his eyes.

Kāʻeo's head was buzzing, but not enough to make him forget about Tūtūpapa. "Wea your phone stay?" Kāʻeo looked around the carpet, ducking down and looking under the couch. He hit Junior's side. "Your phone?"

"Remind me fo spot you one of my extras," Junior told Kāʻeo, passing him his cell phone. Kāʻeo looked down at the screen, the display showing six missed calls. He listened to the voicemails. Tūtūpapa was dying, his father said. Liver cancer. Complications. He was in the emergency room. Queen's. Pops rattled off the room number. The next message was from Mark. "I dunno what da fuck you doing, but you need fo give me one call." He hung up and scrolled through the missed calls, and then dialed Mark's number back. His brother picked up.

"Tell Ma I stay on my way," Kāʻeo said, rushing to find his pants.

"You stay kidding right?" Mark asked, the words coming through heavy and clear. "Dat was how long ago already."

Kāʻeo hesitated to ask. "What about Papa?"

"You really never get any of da messages?" Mark asked. "You really never know what da fuck was going on dis whole time?"

"I going be right dea," Kāʻeo pleaded.

"I told you already," Mark interrupted, putting his brother's negotiation to rest. "He stay gone, Kāʻeo, couple hours now."

Kāʻeo paced back and forth. "What?" he wiped his face. "How?"

Mark hesitated, his exhales coming through the speaker. "Papa been sick one long time, Kāʻeo," Mark conceded. "Not jus da cancer, you understand? You know what I stay talking about?" Kāʻeo stopped, an empty beer bottle lying at his feet. "Fo be honest, I dunno what you stay doing, especially wit one fucking nobody like Junior, but you should have been dea, Kāʻeo, you know dat?" Mark added. His voice elevated. "And I no care what da fuck you get going on, you need fo get your shit straight already, keh? No more bullshit cuz dis stay about more than you right now, ah? You listening to me or what?"

"Yah," Kāʻeo finally said.

"I get shit fo do, my own shit fo take care of, I no need…" Mark stopped himself. "Nevermind already, jus get your ass home, keh?" he said, and then hung up.

Kāʻeo stood there holding the phone. Tūtūpapa was dead. He had been sick for a long time. *Not jus da cancer, you understand? You know what I stay talking about?* "Fuck," Kāʻeo said, picking up the empty bottle from the floor. "Fuck," he whispered to himself.

Kā'eo spent the weeks leading up to his grandfather's funeral in a stupor, numb with grief. He tried to call his mother, but every time she answered, he sat there, speechless, still struggling with Tūtūpapa's death. Finally, Pops called to remind Kā'eo about the arrangements for the next day, to let him know that the family expected him to be there. "I need fo talk wit you," Kā'eo spit out, nervous to finally face him. "Tonight."

When he got there, Pops was sitting in the driveway with a plastic chair next to him. Kā'eo expected his hands to be slick with salt, to feel his stomach twisting down, but he was calm, his forehead dry. A termite landed on the nape of Kā'eo's neck and he swatted it without thinking. "Fucking things," he waved another one away.

"You always hated termite season," Pops remarked, offering his son a silver can from the cooler, the streetlight glistening off of it in streams.

Kā'eo took it without thinking, knowing that he had a long night ahead of him. "Give me one reason we need da fuckahs," Kā'eo challenged his father, pressing the tab back and taking a long draw.

"You got me," Pops conceded. He glanced at Kā'eo and watched him drink, examining his son's fingernails, his wrists, the untouched stretch of flesh running up his forearm, his cheeks and lips.

"Howz Ma?" Kā'eo asked, trying to ease the tension between them, watching a termite crawling across the cooler lid.

"Some nights are better than others, but she's going to get through it. We all will," Pops added, encouraged by Kā'eo's presence. He leaned forward in his chair and looked at Kā'eo, noticing the soft slope of his mother's shoulders in his sons. "And what about you, how are you doing with all of this? To be honest, I didn't think it would take you this long."

"Okay," Kāʻeo lied, to his father and to himself, the termite gone for the moment. "Jus trying fo get through, you know? Jus trying fo understand."

Pops nodded. "I don't think there's a good answer for that either," he said. "One day everything was fine, and then…" Kāʻeo opened his mouth in skepticism, but then closed the gap with another drink. "How's school?" Pops asked.

"Da same," Kāʻeo saw no reason to worry him.

"You working?"

"Looking right now," Kāʻeo replied. It wasn't that far from the truth. Once he had a better handle on things, once everything had settled down, he would be. "Trying fo decide what I like do," he added. Better, he told himself.

Pops treaded carefully. "And you're staying at your friend's place, right?"

Kāʻeo looked at his father, sure that Mark had said something about Junior's reputation after hearing about where Kāʻeo had been spending his time. "Had one apartment in town, but with everything going on, you know? Never make sense fo hold on to da place."

Pops continued his inquiry. "He's a friend of yours from high school, right?"

"Das right," Kāʻeo nodded, keeping his father at a comfortable distance.

"We ever meet him?" Pops tried to be nonchalant. "I mean I remember a couple of your—"

"Nah," Kāʻeo cut him off.

"Good guy?" Pops didn't give up.

But Kāʻeo was losing his patience with the topic. "I dunno what you wen hear, Pops. I dunno what Mark wen tell you," he corrected himself, "but Junior not li'dat."

"So no drugs then?" Pops matched his son's approach, figuring he had already been found out anyway. "Just two friends hanging out, having a good, clean time?"

"I came hea fo talk about Papa, I never come fo one interrogation, or one fucking intervention, or whatever. If you get da shrink waiting in da garage, can tell her come out already, I going tell her da same shit."

"We're just curious, that's all. Concerned," Pops assured his son. "Things are bad enough as it is right now."

"You no think I know dat?" Kā'eo threw a look at his father.

"Then answer the question," Pops pushed.

"I knew dis was going happen, you know dat?" Kā'eo parried. "Jus like wit 'awa. You guys get one idea in your head and you no can see straight. You already get your minds made up das why, so no need give me one chance fo say my piece, ah? Stay like dis," he raised his beer, waving it in the streetlight. "Nobody like raise one stink wen came to da real problem in dis family, but wen came to 'awa..." Kā'eo stopped himself. "I mean fucking look at us."

"Mark tell you?" Pops asked, putting his can down.

"No need," Kā'eo replied. "But I thought he was done wit all dat."

"It doesn't matter," Pops dismissed Kā'eo's remark. "And I hope that you know we were always happy with what you were doing, you know, learning the language, the culture." Pops put a hand on his son's arm. "Your grandfather too."

"You no need do dat, you know," Kā'eo dismissed his father's effort. "Papa never care about what I was doing, not really. He wen see things different, you guys wen see things different, and das alright, but no need bullshit me now jus cuz Papa not hea anymore. Jus be straight wit me, you know, jus be honest. I hea fo talk, das all, so no need apologize."

"He was proud that you were in college, that you were doing as well as you were," Pops said. "Doing as well you are," he corrected himself, giving his son the benefit of the doubt. "Your grandfather, all of us, we just tried to do what was best," Pops said. "For you and for your brothers. We raised you the best way we knew how."

"I know dat."

"He loved you."

"I know dat too."

"So what then?" his father pushed.

"Was never about dat," Kā'eo began, catching one of the termites, examining it in his palm. "Stay about, I dunno, dat feeling of being hea and not knowing who you stay." The termite's wings fluttered, its body twitched. "You go college wit fuckahs who can trace their whole histories back, can chant their mo'olelo mo'okū'auhau from memory.

But me, all I know is da kine: fo sing *Hawai'i Pono'i* wit my Pidgin tongue and my English first name. *Robert,* dey wen call me, and I tell dem jus like I wen tell Haywood or any of da oddah fuckahs in high sku: *Kā'eo,* like I really wen know what dat name means," Kā'eo said, wiping the termite's carcass off on his shorts. "And you know, I know you guys was looking out fo me but…" He took a moment to articulate the right words, taking a drink. "Dat no mean you guys was right fo how crazy you guys wen ack. I mean, we stay family, right, blood, why I need fo earn da right fo choose how I like live my life? Why I need fo define my Hawaiianness on your guys' terms?" Kā'eo ran his fingers over his sandpaper cheeks and then down to his chin, tracing his jawline. He recalled the image of his granduncle on his corkboard, the stranger with the same heavy jaw. "But like I said already, I not hea fo one apology, I hea fo understand, you know?" Kā'eo said. "Why all of a sudden, huh? What wen happen dis time?" It was the one thing that he couldn't figure out and that Mark had failed to tell him.

"It doesn't matter," Pops said honestly.

"Maybe you right," Kā'eo nodded. "But maybe not, you know? Maybe I jus like know, yah, fo myself. Fo help me get through dis."

"He had been sober for twenty years, Kā'eo," Pops said. "It was always a struggle for him."

"I know about dat Thanksgiving, Pop. Da way Papa was acking, how Ma and him was fighting, all da shit about Danny boy. I dunno if dea was any oddah times, but I know about dat." Kā'eo had spent days wading through his memories: holidays, special occasions, birthdays. If he went deep enough, he might remember a dark kitchen, the cap of a whiskey bottle loosening, or the tinkle of ice against glass, his grandfather's hands shaking. But he could never be sure.

"Your mother kept track of him. He went to his meetings, he went to church, he was doing good for a long time."

"Das what I saying, so what wen happen den?" Kā'eo continued his inquiry. In his mind, he could almost make out the wear on his grandfather's cross. "Why all of a sudden?"

Pops took a large draw from his can. "You should really talk to your mother about this," Pops told him, not fully prepared to discuss the topic with him any further.

Kāʻeo was honest. "I no like talk about dis wit her," he said. "She been through enough already, and I know how she going ack."

Pops nodded. His son was right. "He'd been having a hard time," Pops said, getting it out as best he could. "You know that already."

"Cuz of Uncle Joseph, cuz of Danny boy," Kāʻeo finished Pops' rationale before his father could make it more than it was. "But dat was years ago too."

Pops opened his mouth to answer but dug in the pocket of his jeans instead. He pulled out a key ring. He held it out for Kāʻeo, the keys dancing in the streetlight. "Because of this," Pops said, handing the keys to him. "Because he wasn't been able to do more with it than pay for the storage unit it's sitting in." Pops told him where. "He wanted you to have it."

Kāʻeo took it from him and ran his fingers over the blemishes in the metal, picking at the rust with his thumbnail. He recalled the photograph that he had found in the box that Tūtūpapa had given him: Tūtūpapa and Uncle Joseph, his brother, smiling in front of a beat up hull. "Why?" Kāʻeo asked, not sure of what to make of the inheritance.

"The boat was theirs," Pops did his best to explain. "Your Papa's and your granduncle's. They were building it together, and then everything happened between them, and your uncle just didn't want anything to do with your grandfather anymore."

"And what?"

"Your uncle's wife tried to give it to Tūtūpapa, but he didn't want it," Pops paused. "He couldn't take it, I guess," he said, making sure his explanation was as close to the facts as it could be. "So it became your cousin's, but when Danny died, he left it to your grandfather."

"I still no understand," Kāʻeo looked at his father.

"What did Papa tell you about what happened between the two of them?" Pops asked.

Kāʻeo reached for another beer. "Nutten," he answered truthfully, his suspicions about his grandfather's explanation coming back. "Ma said dey wen lose touch, dat dey never really wen resolve things."

Pops stopped him, resting a hand on the cooler lid. "I shouldn't be talking about this," Pops told Kāʻeo. "This is not what I wanted to talk about tonight."

Kāʻeo was starting to feel the buzz of the alcohol, a dizziness coming over him. "No give me dat," Kāʻeo replied.

"And you should slow down," Pops added.

"No more bullshit, Pop."

"Your uncle, he just—" Pops sputtered. "Between prison and everything else."

"Jus spit um out," Kāʻeo pushed.

"He just couldn't live with it anymore," Pops said it quickly, not knowing how else to make it clear. "And your grandfather, he—" Pops hesitated. He could see Kāʻeo's face twisting in the streetlight. "It's like your mother told you, they never resolved things, and your Papa—" Pops stopped himself from going any further. "It was just one of those things," he backtracked. "Family's complicated," he began again. "And you know how your grandfather was, he carried his family on his back, every success, every mistake." He looked at his son. "And when he found out about the cancer," Pops squeezed his son's hand. "He was just sorry for how he left it with you, he never forgave himself for that night, and he hoped—"

But Kāʻeo wasn't listening to his father anymore. Kāʻeo looked down at the key in the streetlight, realizing now what his grandfather must have called to tell him. And what had he done: swore at him, hung up the phone, not even given a shit, while he was on the other end, dying. "How long after?" Kāʻeo asked, needing to know for sure. "Was what, not even one month?"

"And you know you're right," Pops admitted, attempting to derail his son's train of thought. "We could have done more with you. We could have tried to get you in a better school."

"Fuck," Kāʻeo leaned forward and held back the sick in his stomach. "Dat night, I never even mean dat shit, you know? I was jus tired, I was jus pissed off, so much shit going on."

"Papa, too, he could have taught you how to throw net like his father did. He could have tried to teach you more about that side of the family, about his cousins on Kauaʻi and Molokaʻi. He could have done better, we all could have done better," Pops hammered out his concession. "But we always loved you," Pops told Kāʻeo, but his words were just background noise now. "You know, that's—" Pops licked his lips and took a breath. "He told me to tell you that, Papa wanted to make sure that you knew."

Kāʻeo started to choke, the alcohol burning up his throat. "I never fucking mean any of dat shit," he stammered. "Why you guys let me say dat shit to him? Why you guys jus wen sit dea?"

"Take it easy," his father rubbed his back. "Breathe, Kāʻeo. Listen to me, to what I'm telling you."

"I wen call him one coward," Kāʻeo spit up. "I wen call him one traitor."

"It was a fight," Pops consoled him. "He was sick, he had been for some time, no one knew."

"I wen call him one disgrace."

"Kā—"

"I never know." Kāʻeo looked up at the streetlight and swallowed hard, biting his tongue to distract him from the taste of his own bile, suddenly aware of his father's hand on his back, Pops' face close to his. Fuck, he wanted to scream. "Fuck," he did. "Why you never say something?" he asked his father. "Dat night, dis whole time."

Pops swallowed his response. "This is not your fault, Kāʻeo," Pops said earnestly. "You need to understand that."

But it didn't matter. Kāʻeo was done denying what he had suspected all along. He was surprised by how much of it had already eaten away at him, the remains of his guilt coming up in his gut, but he accepted his actions for what they were. "And I never even wen have da decency fo be dea fo him," Kāʻeo admitted. "Mark stay right, I was all wrapped up in my own stupid shit, I never care about you guys, about what da fuck was going on hea. I never care about nutten but myself."

Pops put an arm around Kāʻeo's back. "It's been a long night, we should go inside, rest a little while, we've got a long day tomorrow."

Kāʻeo blinked, still gripping the chair. "I no think..." he mumbled.

"I'm going to wake up early, make some eggs, deviled ham, and potatoes."

"I got to go," Kāʻeo said, his stomach still turning. "I no can be hea right now."

"You can't drive like this," Pops told him. "You can sleep here and go get ready in the morning."

"I not ready fo stay hea, no deserve fo stay hea," Kāʻeo replied. His vision was spotted, but that much was clear.

"You're not making any sense," Pops reasoned with his son.

Kāʻeo wanted desperately to agree with his father, but it was too late now. "You no understand," Kāʻeo let go. "I wen do dis, me," he slapped his chest. "I stay da reason he stay dead right now."

"No," Pops shook Kāʻeo. "This is not your fault. This is no one's fault. You need to understand that. You need to remember that," he pleaded, but his son was somewhere else.

Remember what I wen tell you long time ago? Kāʻeo looked up, he could hear his grandfather's voice, *Pūpūkahi i holomua.* Kāʻeo stared up at the streetlight. *You remember dat, Kāʻeo?* And then he felt it, the sudden gasp of memory:

The moment was a wave long since receded, the passing of time and tide having pushed it deep into the depths of Kāʻeo's experiences, but it had always been with him. Kāʻeo was ten years old, standing with Tūtūpapa on the shore at Kualoa, the two of them watching a group of paddlers heading out. "Pūpūkahi i holomua," one of them called out. "Pūpūkahi i holomua," they all responded in unison.

"What dey saying, Papa?" Kāʻeo had asked his grandfather.

"Unite fo move forward," Tūtūpapa translated for him. "If you like get wea you need fo go, everybody need fo work together." Kāʻeo looked out at the paddlers, several of them were larger than the others, while some were quicker and more agile with the paddles in their hands. "Das how life stay, you understand? If you no work together, you jus going be stuck in one place, going around in circles, you know?" Tūtūpapa explained. "Stay about seeing past yourself, ah?"

Kāʻeo looked around. "Huh?"

Tūtūpapa smiled. "Stay like one family, everybody get one job, ah?" he tried to make it clearer for his grandson. "Your parents take care of you and your braddahs, and das their job. You go sku and help wit your braddahs, and das your job. And hopefully all you guys going grow up, and den wen your parents need you guys, or you need your braddahs, or your braddahs need you, den you going be dea, you understand?

Family takes care, and wen family no take care you take care cuz you can, you understand?"

Kāʻeo smiled at Tūtūpapa's puzzle. "Oddahwise lickens?" he finally asked, confident in his response.

"Oddahwise nobody going nowea," Tūtūpapa told him. "Oddahwise everybody end up in da water bumbai."

"Pupuahi e holonua," Kāʻeo said.

"Pūpūkahi i holomua," Tūtūpapa corrected his grandson. "No forget."

"Pūpūkahi i holomua," Kāʻeo said to his father, finally realizing what Tūtūpapa was trying to remind him of that night. He looked down at his hand, at the smear of termite on his palm. He was no longer shaking. "Stay one Hawaiian proverb," Kāʻeo continued to explain. "Everybody on da waʻa working as one team, as one unit, as one family."

"I don't understand," Pops said, not following his son's logic.

"Das what Papa was trying fo tell me, but I never like listen, and you know why?" Kāʻeo swallowed again, and then let it go: "What stay my purpose, Pops? What I been good fo all these years except fo headaches and bullshit?"

"Come on," Pops stood up and tried to pull Kāʻeo out of his seat.

He resisted. "You know why I hate termites, Pops? Why da fuckahs bug da shit out of me?" Kāʻeo looked up at the streetlight, the termites still lingering on the lens. He thought about his family and his friends, and all of the choices that he had made for himself, not thinking about anyone else. "Cuz da only thing dey stay good fo is nutten. Dey consume. Dey destroy. Da homes you build up, dey eat away at all da supports until all you get left is da empty parts."

"Like I told you, this was nobody's fault," Pops pleaded. "We all wish things had been different, but in the end, we have to accept what we can't control."

But his father was wrong. "No spit dat church bullshit to me. Forgiveness stay fo fuckahs who still get one chance, but I no can go back now," Kāʻeo said, his actions finally making sense to him. "One natural order, how things work. Termites, dey not around all da time, yah? Always get one season. You fix what you can, you build da house up again, but until you tent dat fuckah, dey always going be waiting, ready fo fuck things up one more time, jus like me, jus like I been doing dis whole time."

"We don't give up on family, Kāʻeo, you know that," Pops shook his head.

"Das how, Pop, jus like Papa, jus like ʻohana stay one magic word or something. Like dat really going change shit, like da whole world going be different, everything going look brighter, everything going have one purpose again. I love you Pop, I love Ma, too. Mark one good kid, he still get one chance. Elani smart, I hope he no end up like me. But Papa stay fucking dead already and dat shit stay on me, nobody else. ʻohana not going bring him back."

Pops opened his mouth to say something but stopped himself. He stuffed his hands in his pockets and then walked out to the curb and stood in the flicker of the streetlamp. "Kāʻeo," Pops said, drawing from his own recollections. "Years ago, you wanted to know why we gave it to you, where it came from."

"Was Nana's faddah's name. Righteous, full of knowledge," Kāʻeo recited the definition, word for word.

"It was the name Papa wanted to give his son, if he had had one," Pops said, the wind passing over them. "That's why we gave it to you."

Kāʻeo thought he could make out the smell of rain. "So dramatic, Pops," he told him, dismissing his father's sentiment.

"Maybe," his father said without taking his eyes off of his son. "It's just one of those things you worry about when you get to my age. Too many folks with too little time, forgetting to say what they really think. I'd hate for you not to know."

"Das what you was really thinking?"

"I was thinking it's time to go inside, you should come in, too," Pops advised. "Your mother already made up your bed."

"You go," Kāʻeo insisted. "I stay good right hea."

"I'll leave the light on for you, then." His father picked up the cooler and carried it up to the porch. When he reached the screen door, he opened it and then looked back at Kāʻeo. "Your mother will be glad to see you tomorrow. Your brothers, too."

Kāʻeo didn't respond, he just stared off, and eventually he heard the screen door close and his father's footsteps disappear. The streetlight above him flickered a few times before becoming a dull glow, a muted orange hue like the reflection of a lighted buoy on the ocean's surface. He leaned back in his chair, and let himself drift off.

He never really dreamed anymore, but tonight he fell asleep and dreamt of termites. He could see them landing on his legs and face, crawling up his arms, and migrating to him as if he were a piece of driftwood washed up on the shore. They went into his ears, his nose, and all the tiny places that he could not see. It was there, inside him, that they made their home. They fed on whatever they could find and only after they had riddled his body with tunnels and holes did they disappear, leaving him with no memory of his body or his name.

When Kāʻeo woke up, he was lying on the concrete, his chair on its side. How long he had been out, he wasn't sure. The streetlamp had stopped flickering and the street was a deep black. Mark's truck was home. Kāʻeo stumbled up off the ground, his knees almost buckling when he tried to move. He made his way up the walkway and to the porch. Kāʻeo wondered what Mark would say if he walked through the door, would he look at him with animosity and shame or greet him like the brothers that they were? What Elani going say? Ma? It was then that Kāʻeo noticed the scattered collection of wings on the screen. He tried to brush them away, the remnants falling like tears. He rested his face against the frame, the wings clinging to his cheeks. He turned away, not willing to take the risk.

Kāʻeo made his way down the driveway and stopped near Mark's truck. Mark had left his window open. Kāʻeo dug in his pockets and pulled out the key ring his father had given him and left the keys on the dash. He walked down to his own truck and got in.

He leaned back in the driver's seat and tried to focus in on the alcohol, the buzz that was leaving him, but he knew that it would never be enough. On the floor, he could see the glint of a glass pipe, the bulb nestled between the pages of his grandfather's obituary. He looked in the rear-view mirror, and for a moment, he was suddenly overcome with optimism: that things could be different, that there was a chance, that if he just got out, his grandfather would be standing there on the porch, waiting for him. But that's all it was, fleeting hope, with no other lights left on the street that night except for the flicker from his lighter, the bulb filling him with a strange but familiar warmth, pulling him further and further down.

Mark

Heaha ka hala i kapuhia ai ka leo, i hoʻokuli mai ai?
What was the wrong that forbade the voice, that caused the deafness?

Proverb 509, Pukui 61

When Mark found out that Kāʻeo had left the house, he was ecstatic. Mark had gone his whole childhood taking Kāʻeo's orders and waiting his turn: because Kāʻeo was older, because Kāʻeo was more responsible. *Because I wen put him in charge,* Ma would say, but all Mark would hear was: cuz I not him. So when he walked into Kāʻeo's room, he saw all the scraps that he had missed out on because he had come second to the table. His brother's privilege and independence captured in that single space. Mark immediately grabbed his stereo and his comedy CDs, prioritizing the rest of his belongings by need and transporting them across the hall.

"No even think about switching rooms," Ma warned Mark mid-move. Switching? Mark was confused; there was no switch involved. "He stay gone already." Mark moved to one of the drawers and pulled it out, displaying the cavity, "Look."

Ma thought nothing of Mark's demonstration. "He jus stay all hardhead right now, das all," Ma told Mark. "And I no think you like him come home and throw your stuff out in da hallway, ah? So either move everything back now or I going move um fo you, and you not going like dat, you understand? Cuz stay hard fo me tell trash from treasure sometimes."

Mark wasn't surprised by his mother's rationale. He thought he had a better chance with his father. "Pop," Mark said, walking into the kitchen, where his father was emptying grocery bags from the store.

"You heard your mother, Mark," Pops dismissed his son's attempt before Mark even began.

"Dis stay fucking ridiculous, you know dat?" Mark argued. "I get one life too, you know? I come home from work all tired, ready fo relax, and I have fo deal wit Elani on his computer screen all night or his damn reading light in my face."

"Your brother has school," Pops told him. "If you have a problem with it, ask him if he can turn it off or ask him to read in the living room."

"Das not da point," Mark countered. "Kāʻeo been in and out of hea fo months now, doing whatever da fuck he wants, and dat damn room jus sitting dea."

"It's still his room, Mark," Pops didn't budge. "Like your mother said, how would you like it if you came home and Elani had moved all of your stuff out?"

"Good, dat means I get da oddah room to myself."

"That's not what I meant and you know it."

Mark paced back and forth in the dining room. "What about wen Lana comes over, huh? You know how da kine dat stay wit Elani over in da corner? You like me ask him fo cover his eyes?"

"You know you not allowed fo be alone in your room wit her," Ma reminded Mark, making the sign of the cross.

"I stay nineteen, Ma," Mark shook his head at her gesture. "And believe me, if I like have sex, I no need fo do um hea."

"Marcelo Kekoa Teixeira, Jr.," Ma stood up, tired of arguing. "I no need dis right now. You like waste your energy, das fine, but dis topic not up for discussion, you understand?"

"I stay done wit dis already," Mark started for the hallway. "You know what," he stopped. "Maybe I going move out too, you know? I get one savings. I stay making enough money fo afford one place on my own."

Pops didn't like where this was going. "That money is for when you really need it," Pops lectured Mark. "For when you want to buy a place, or you know," Pops looked up at his son, "when you decide to go back to school and you need to take a break from working."

Mark laughed. "I no see you talking to Kāʻeo about what da fuck he doing wit his time or his money, but wen comes to me, yah, everybody get one opinion."

"You know that's not true," Pops replied.

"Whatever."

"Like your mother said, your brother just needs a few days."

"Well what about what I need, huh?" Mark slapped his chest.

"Tell you what," Pops threw a glance at Ma. "Give him to March, okay? If he's still adamant about doing things on his own, the room is yours."

"Now, I dunno…" Ma waved her finger in the air.

"Marcy," Pops looked at her. Ma stared strong, but eventually conceded with a nod and sat back down. "One month," Pops said to Mark, "okay?" Mark couldn't wait.

But by the time March came around, Kāʻeo's room was the last thing on Mark's mind. The whole family woke up to the rattle of the screen door, someone banging on the metal frame. When Mark came out of his room, he saw Tūtūpapa standing in the entranceway, his cheekbones washed in yellow light, and then his grandfather collapsed in Ma's arms and started to sob. Even from the hallway, the alcohol stung the edges of Mark's nostrils. Ma got Tūtūpapa a glass of water and made up Kāʻeo's bed. "We going have one talk in da morning," Mark heard Ma tell Tūtūpapa, and then went to bed.

Tūtūpapa was sick, dying. "How long you wen know?" Ma asked him. "How come you never wen say something?" Mark was out in the lānai, cleaning his work boots.

"I never like worry nobody," he said, his voice raspy and dry.

"So what, you jus wen decide fo drink yourself to death?"

"Kāʻeo not hea?" Tūtūpapa stood up, suddenly aware that he was in his grandson's room. Mark heard the bed springs. "Das what I came hea fo, fo talk wit him."

Mark could tell by Ma's hesitation that it was a topic that she was not keen to discuss. "He still gone," Ma said. "Guess he doing okay."

"You wen talk to him?"

"Not fo one while," Ma replied. "Why, he wen call you?"

"I wen call him," Tūtūpapa admitted, unsure of how long it had been. "After I wen find out."

"And what?"

"Das all," Tūtūpapa said. "Was one short talk." He didn't divulge anything more than that.

Ma must have understood. She got up and opened the bedroom door. "Come, I know you hungry," she told Tūtūpapa. "Can talk more later," she said, and then the two of them left for the kitchen.

Before Mark went inside, he walked out to the far end of the backyard, out of earshot of the lānai. Although Mark could care less where his brother was, he thought that Kāʻeo at least deserved to know that their grandfather was sick. Three rising tones and a recorded message: "We're sorry, you have reached a number that has been disconnected or is no longer in service." Mark hung up and dialed again. Same recording. Whatever his brother was doing, he hoped that it was worth it.

Tūtūpapa's condition quickly worsened. Neither Ma or Pops could afford to take a leave of absence, so they relied on Mark to take Tūtūpapa to his radiation therapy when they couldn't. Mark rearranged his schedule with his job, taking on security shifts on nights and weekends, leaving his weekdays open to take his grandfather to Queen's. He also started to take on more responsibility at home, preparing dinners in advance for his parents, taking care of other chores around the house, and making sure that Elani was alright. But the additional responsibilties came at a cost for Mark, and his girlfriend, Lana, was growing concerned.

They were on Mark's lunch hour, Korean food on the bench outside his security booth. "You're doing too much, you know that?" she had told him. The days were wearing on him, she could tell by how thin he looked and the shadows under his eyes. He looked like he was in costume, wearing an older skin.

"I need fo take care, you know dat."

"You need a break," she said, picking at her vegetable plate, "that's what I know."

"Das what we doing, right?" Mark speared a shoyu potato.

"Be serious for once," she told him.

"Papa's cancer not going take one break. My parents no can afford fo take one break. So I not going take one break, you know?" Mark nodded to the rhytmn of his words.

"So you're just going to keep killing yourself then?" Lana asked, not bothering to finish. She closed her plate up and threw it in the trash.

"Das da plan," Mark joked, shoveling a helping of rice in his mouth.

"For how long?"

"Fo as long as I need to."

"And what about us, I thought you wanted to find a place?" Lana continued her inquiry. "What about going back to school, about getting your degree, do you want to keep working security the rest of your life?"

"No," Mark admitted. "But all dat can wait, ah? Dis no can."

Lana shook her head. "It's not going to get easier, you know that right?"

"Das why I stay doing what I can," he closed his plate, "now."

But she knew Mark better than that. "I think this is about more than that."

"No get all da kine on me, psycho-social whatevers," he said, before Lana could lecture him on another study about birth-order. "Dis stay about family, das all. About my responsibility to dem. You think I like feeling like I one zombie all da time?"

"Then why do you do it?" Lana countered. "You don't need to take on everything."

Mark looked at his watch. "You stay acking ridiculous right now, you know dat?"

"That's okay," she told him. "You don't need to admit it to me, but don't act like I'm crazy."

He pecked her lips. "You not one psychologist yet, you know dat?"

"You're barely around, Mark." She kissed him again. "I just miss you and I'm tired of seeing you so drained."

"Maybe you right," he nodded. "I going talk to my folks, see what stay going on. Even if no can cut back, maybe can take one weekend off, stay in Waikīkī. Our anniversary stay coming up."

"Even a day for yourself is a step forward," Lana told him. "At least it would give you some time to recharge."

He agreed. And the next day, when his parents got off of work, he sat them both down and told them just that. "We appreciate all of your help, you know that," Pops acknowledged Mark's efforts.

But Ma was another story, between Tūtūpapa's diagnosis and Kāʻeo's absence, the stress and anxiety was getting to her more than anyone else. "Das not what dis stay about," she hopped off the couch. "Dis not about stress, we all stay stressed, you not da only one."

"I know dat, Ma," Mark agreed. "I jus wen figure, you know, Papa no need go hospital on da weekends and I get one vacation coming up wit my job."

"You like book one hotel and go fool around wit your girlfriend, den go," she said.

"Ma," Mark backtracked.

"Marcy," Pops put a hand on her back to calm her.

"Like I said, not like you guys need me on da weekends," Mark appealed to her. "And wen I stay hea, you know I stay doing everything I can fo Papa, fo you guys."

"And what about your braddah?" Ma snapped. "What you stay doing fo him?"

Mark found her question odd. When Elani needed a ride somewhere, Mark took him. When Elani needed money, Mark was more than willing to open his wallet. Perhaps Mark's only sin was that he let Elani stay on the computer all day instead of pushing him to get out of the house. "Elani doing fine," Mark told her. "Well," he cracked, looking to make sure that his younger brother wasn't around, "he doing fine fo Elani."

"Das right," Ma raised her eyebrows and her finger at her son. "Make your jokes, ack all da kine, but while you stay out in Waikīkī wit dat floozy of one girlfriend, you think about wea your braddah stay. How he prolly out dea on da streets by himself."

Then he realized whom she was talking about. "You kidding me, right?"

"You da one making jokes, not me," Ma told him.

"He stay twenty-one years old, what da hell you like me do? He no even get da sense fo pay his damn phone bill."

Ma's eyes searched the room, darting back and forth in her head. "You never care," Ma said. She sat and started to rub her forehead. "As soon as he was out of dis house, you was trying fo take his room. You never care, you never like him come back home."

Mark was beyond patience, the blood rushing to his temples. "Everything I stay doing," he huffed.

"See, he no listen," Ma said to Pops, breaking Mark out of his recollection. "I stay trying fo talk sense to him and he no even care."

"It's okay," Pops told him. "Do what you need to, take the weekend, whatever you need." He pulled Ma close to him and buried her head in his chest. "Don't worry about your mother."

It wasn't worry or concern that was getting to him, it was resentment surging through his bloodstream again. Mark recalled the time that he and Kāʻeo were in the yard when they were kids. Elani was still in elementary school then. Mark was picking guavas in the grass while Kāʻeo worked in the rocks closest to the house. Mark was focused on his work, picking with one hand, dragging his bucket with the other. When Ma came out to check on them, Mark was ready to hold his bucket up with pride, but when he turned around he found a scatter of rotten fruit across the grass; Kāʻeo smiling from under the tree, his hand steadying the lowest branch.

Mark balled his fist up like a child and huffed. "No fucking talk to me," he told her and then marched down the hallway. "I no like hear shit about Kāʻeo anymore," he yelled.

When Mark got to his room, he wasn't surprised to see Elani at his desk, working away at his keyboard. Mark envied Elani's ability to lose himself. The world could be drowning outside their window, and Elani would be more concerned with the pages that he had left to write or read. Mark laid down and closed his eyes, waiting for his pulse to settle. The click of keys came to a stop.

"Are you going to go?" Elani asked him, his attention still on the screen in front of him. "Move out or whatever?"

Mark opened his eyes and laced his hands behind his head. "I dunno, I stay fucking tired of Ma's bullshit already."

"You think something's wrong with her?" Elani asked. "You think she's sick?"

"In da head maybe," Mark joked.

Elani didn't laugh. "What about Kāʻeo?"

"You think I know? You think I give a shit?" Mark replied. He turned to look at Kāʻeo's bedroom door and caught a glimpse of the faded scar running from his right bicep and down his arm. "You know how he stay, wen he stay all one way about something, das all he care about." Mark thought about the times that he and Kāʻeo had raced at Kualoa: the moment Kāʻeo got ahead, all his brother could think about was pressing forward, never worrying about Mark, no matter how far behind Mark fell. "He no give a shit about nobody or nutten, jus himself."

Elani didn't respond. He went back to typing, his fingers composing a fractured string of clicks and clacks. Mark closed his eyes again, imagining that the sound was rain hitting the jalousies, an uneven pitter-pack, the kind that always came before the sun crept through the screen. In his mind he could almost feel it: the heat on his skin, Lana lying beside him in the sand, the hum of Waikīkī enveloping them.

"I hope you stay," Elani told him. "At least until things settle down."

Mark was surprised by the concern in his brother's tone. It was unlike Elani to let his emotions show. "I going try," he promised him, not knowing what else to say. "I going try."

And Mark did his best to keep that promise to Elani, but as Tūtūpapaʻs condition spiraled so did the situation at home. June came, and with it a flood that blanketed the Windward side for a month. Summer meant Ma had more time to dwell on problems at home, with school out and not starting up again until the end of July. Pops' construction job ended, and then work stalled; he took jobs when they came up, but for the most part, he was home. When Mark wasn't at work or with Lana, he had to find other ways to keep from listening to the two of them fighting about bills, about the house, and about Kāʻeo.

But he could never fully avoid the tension. Any time he left, he could feel his mother's eyes on him, interrogating his intent. And when he came home, she would often be sitting in the dark, watching the clock. Mark felt guilty about it, but when he was at home, he found himself using Elani's computer to check Craigslist, looking for a place that he and Lana could make their own, someplace far from Kahaluʻu.

"She's just worried about your grandfather," Pops would rationalize. "And about your brother, she just wants him home before it's too late."

"And what, she need fo take dat out on all of us?" Mark argued.

"You know she doesn't mean it," Pops told him.

"You sure about dat?"

Pops nodded. "I'm sure she loves you," Pops said. "And that she wants you to be happy."

Mark almost laughed. "I dunno how long I can stick around, Pop. I hea fo you guys, but all dis jus stay getting fo be too much already." He felt selfish for saying it, but he owed his father the truth.

"I know," Pops assured him. "But things will get better."

"How you know?"

Pops didn't bother to hide his doubt. "I don't," he said. "But you've just got to trust me." Mark gave his father that.

And then it happened. Three days after Tūtūpapa went in for his monthly scan, the doctors gave him the news: they would be stopping treatment. The cancer had become unresponsive and was spreading rapidly. Ma insisted that he stay with them, but Tūtūpapa was adamant about staying at his own house that night.

Mark listened to the two of them arguing, his grandfather almost unrecognizable:

His skin was pale and his body was hunched and worn. "And what?" Tūtūpapa told her, not a trace of fear in his voice. "Stay nutten dey can do, Marcy, nutten," he pleaded. "For four months I been fighting fo what? Fo wake up every morning, feeling like I no can walk five feet witout falling over." He took a breath, his vocal cords wheezing. "Fo puke my stomach out every time I eat. Fo bleed every time I shit. Fo sit up at night every night wondering if tomorrow going be da day, huh? Fo go church and see da looks on everybody's faces, da apologies and da condolences, like I stay dead already." He licked his lips, his tongue rolling over the cracks. "So, forgive me if I like be by myself tonight. Forgive me if I like sit in my bedroom and think about your grandmaddah and da life I wen have, and how much I love my family." He put a hand on his chest. "Forgive me if I like have one more night fo myself." Ma knew better, but she gave in anyway, certain that she would regret it soon enough.

Mark was with Lana when he got the call. His parents had driven down to check on Tūtūpapa, and when he didn't answer the door, they went inside and found that he had locked himself in his bedroom. The paramedics found him in bed, his morphine prescription and a bottle of vodka on the side table, both of them emptied. They were just lucky that they had gotten there when they did.

When Mark and Lana got to the hospital, Tūtūpapa was barely conscious. "Sorry," Mark told his parents. "We wen leave right wen you guys called." Mark kissed his grandfather's forehead and then grabbed a chair for Lana and for himself.

Ma held tight to one of the chairs. "You mind standing, we stay waiting fo my son," Ma told Lana.

Mark threw a glance at his father. "You not serious?" Mark remarked.

Pops took Ma's hand away from the chair. "Please," he told Lana, welcoming her in before Ma could pull away.

"He called the house earlier," Elani explained. "Couple times."

"What?" Mark couldn't believe it. "You talk to him, you know wea he stay?"

Pops shook his head. "He's with a friend, I left a message letting him know what's going on."

"What da fuck he doing?"

"Keep it down," Pops told him. "We don't know, we haven't heard back from him yet."

"You really think you going to?" Mark said sarcastically.

"You think das funny, ah?" Ma snapped at Mark. "Well, you must be in one joking mood, bringing your girlfriend hea instead of your braddah." She turned her attention to Lana. "No disrespect, but dis stay one family matter, you understand?"

"You're right," she replied. "I just wanted to make sure he got here okay, I didn't think it was right for him to drive by himself."

"Well he hea now," Ma made the situation clear.

"I'm going to go," she whispered to Mark.

"Stay," he told her, the word rushing out of his mouth.

"Just call me after," she told Mark, and then she waved a polite goodbye to the rest of the family. Mark excused himself and walked her to the elevator. When he returned, Pops was waiting for him, ready to rattle off another list of excuses for Ma's behavior. "Ma get one problem, you know dat," Mark said as softly as he could manage, pacing up and down the hall.

"Be patient with her," Pops took hold of Mark's shoulders to steady him.

"She needs fo see somebody already," Mark added. "Even Elani thinks so."

"I know," Pops said. "She's talking to Father Dumadag—"

"One shrink," Mark shook his head. "One doctor."

"After things settle down," Pops assured him. "Now come sit," he took Mark's arm.

"She get no right fo talk to Lana li'dat either."

"I know."

"I telling you, Pop," Mark followed his father. "I no care already. Me and Lana we—"

"I know," Pops interrupted Mark before he could finish, walking with him back through the doorway.

Shortly after, the crests on the cardiograph fell flat and Tūtūpapa was gone. They stayed in the room as long as they could, but they couldn't stay no matter how much Ma argued for more time, "What about Kā'eo, he needs fo say goodbye to his Papa?" Pops tried to console her but it was no use.

Mark did what was right. "You get da number?" Mark asked his father, happy to hear his mother's sobbing suddenly pause. "I going try."

"Thank you," Pops said, passing him the scrap of paper.

Mark stepped out into the hallway and dialed. The phone rang but went straight to voicemail. "Eh, you wen reach Junior's voicemail, you know what fo do." *Junior?* "You got to be fucking kidding me," Mark said under his breath. He recognized the voice and the name.

Even when Kā'eo and Junior had been friends in high school, Mark didn't like him. He was a pothead and an asshole. Once, Mark caught a ride with them after school, and even though Mark had told Junior several times to watch his cigarette, a flick of ash always found its way into Mark's left eye. But did Kā'eo say anything? "Jus move to da oddah side and stop crying already," Kā'eo told Mark. Last Mark had seen of Junior, he had gotten caught smoking weed in the bathroom behind the gym and had to transfer schools. But Mark still heard things, and rumor was that Junior had moved on from his stoner days and had started selling ice.

It had to be a mistake. Mark dialed the number again just to be sure. "Eh, you wen—" Mark hit the keypad and skipped straight to the beep. "I dunno what da fuck you doing, but you need fo give me one call," Mark said, and then left his number on the machine.

When Mark got back in the hospital room, he could see the vulnerability in Ma's gaze, the yearning for hope in her stare. And he knew that he if he wanted to, he could easily shoot her down, letting her know exactly whom her golden child had spent his time with. But what good would that do right now? Another argument? Another fight? He looked around the room: Pops trying so hard to hold everything together; Elani sitting with his chin tucked to his chest; Tūtūpapa lying there, gone. "I left him one message," Mark said honestly. "Stay late already, if he never wen get da message yet, prolly not going hear from him until tomorrow."

Ma started to tear up again. "But he needs…"

"He'll get his chance, Marcy," Pops assured her. "I'll make sure he's there."

"You guys go home," Mark told them. "I going wait around jus in case."

And there it was again: Ma raised her head and wiped her cheeks with a tissue. "You sure?" she asked him with gratitude.

"I get dis," Mark promised her. "Go home, get some rest."

After they left, Mark went out to the lobby and waited. He watched the clock, the second hand eating away at his patience. An hour passed, then two. Although he had been open to forgiving Kāʻeo for his absence, he was beginning to feel his animosity for him returning again, this time with fervor, fueled by the knowledge of Kāʻeo's whereabouts. He really no give a shit, Mark shook his head. He no fucking care. Mark pulled out his phone and called Lana. "Can come get me?" he asked her, then walked out to the curb and waited for her to arrive.

Mark didn't hear from Kāʻeo until Lana had already picked him up and dropped him off at home. He tried to remain calm, composed, balancing his anger and frustration with his consideration for Elani, who was passed out on the other side of the room. After Mark hung up, he went out into the living room and waited for his father to wake up. Mark knew that if Kāʻeo still had a chance, Pops would be the only one to get him to see reason. He told his father what he knew, trying his best to stick to the facts. Mark didn't want to scare Pops, but he also wanted to make sure Pops knew exactly the type of people Kāʻeo was associating himself with.

"And you're sure about this?" Pops asked.

"Not really," Mark said. "But if dis stay da same guy, den yah."

"Did he seem out of it?"

"Nah," Mark replied. "He seemed da kine, worried, concerned."

"So you think he's okay?" Pops asked him.

Mark considered the question, doing his best to remain objective. "I think he starting fo realize dat maybe he wen make one mistake," Mark said, remembering how distraught Kāʻeo had been. "I think he starting fo regret what wen happen between him and Papa."

Pops nodded. "That's good," he said. "That's something."

"You going call him?"

"He'll call," Pops said with certainty. "I know he will."

"You sure about dat?"

"I'm not really sure about anything these days," Pops remarked.

"But he still deserves a chance right?" Mark wasn't so sure, but for his father's sake, he agreed.

"I get something else I need fo tell you about," Mark said. "Something I was trying fo tell you in da hospital, and I know dis prolly not da right time, but I like at least let you know: me and Lana, we stay looking fo one place right now."

Pops didn't object. "When?" he asked Mark.

"We never find one yet," Mark clarified. "We looking though."

"When?" Pops asked.

"Maybe one month, maybe two, depends I guess," Mark paused and then let it go. "I no like leave befo Papa's funeral."

"Your mother will appreciate that," Pops told him. "Elani, too."

"So you okay wit dis den?" Mark asked.

"You have your own life right, Mark," Pops said, squeezing his son's shoulder. "I know that." Mark smiled as best he could, the moment bittersweet.

In the weeks that followed, Mark stayed true to his word. He

helped with the funeral arrangements, working out the dates with
the church and contacting the family members that were still around,
leaving Pops to handle Ma and Kāʻeo. By the time Pops finally got
in touch with him, it was the night before the funeral. Mark was
disappointed in his brother, but it wasn't his problem anymore. Soon
enough, he would be out of the house and on his own, making a new
life for himself with a woman that he loved. But still get da funeral,
Mark thought on the drive home from Lana's grandparents' house, not
sure what the next day would bring.

Mark turned up their street and made the left into the driveway,
suddenly jerking his truck to the side when he saw Kāʻeo lying on the
concrete. He got out of his truck and looked around. Their father was
nowhere to be found, but he had clearly been there: two chairs still out,
Kāʻeo's chair toppled over beside him. Mark leaned over and shook his
brother, but Kāʻeo just mumbled and swatted at Mark's efforts. "Get da
fuck up," Mark said, shaking him again. "You no can lie hea all night."
But Kāʻeo refused, curling his body up into a ball. "Up to you," Mark
said, leaving Kāʻeo where he had found him.

When Mark got out of the shower, he heard the sound of Kāʻeo's
truck idling outside. He thought about going out there and flagging him
down, letting him know that he probably shouldn't be driving. But then
he caught a glimpse of his scar in the bathroom mirror, a thick divide
of uneven flesh, and he remembered what it felt like that day out in the
water at Kualoa, when he went under and hit the reef: salt in his throat,
blood in his eyes, lucky that Tūtūpapa had come after them. And then
he thought about how Kāʻeo had spent the last six months, and he wasn't
surprised that Kāʻeo was making the same choices that he had made back
then. Mark walked out to the living room and watched Kāʻeo's tail lights
disappear, and then he went to bed and slept until the morning.

Mark looked down at his grandfather, Tūtūpapa's features frozen in a somber state, made up and posed in his casket. Mark said a prayer out of obligation more than faith and broke away from the procession, joining his father outside. There was a tension between them, an unspoken strain. More than once during Pops' eulogy, Mark saw his father linger on the empty space between Mark and Ma. Even now, Mark knew Pops was waiting for Kāʻeo to pull into the parking lot and wondering why he hadn't yet. "I really thought he was going to show today," Pops said, reading Mark's mind. "You sure, he didn't say anything to you last night?"

"Nah," Mark told his father for the third time that day, failing to mention the keys that he had found on his dashboard. Those he threw in the glove box with the grip of napkins and the CD cases that never made their way to the floorboard. "I think you guys jus need fo let him be already," Mark reasoned. "Worry about Ma, worry about Elani."

"We all grieve in our own ways," Pops told Mark.

Mark knew that it was the priest's words and not his father's. "Why he not hea den?" Mark asked honestly. He looked back inside the church at his mother, the day having drained her shaking frame, "Fo Ma at least."

"He has his reasons, Mark," Pops replied, wanting to be just as honest with his son. "I'm not saying that they make much sense, but what does nowadays? We just need to be patient, be open."

"Fo how long?" Mark crossed his arms.

"He's family, Mark," Pops replied, ending their conversation there and heading back inside. "You need to remember that." Mark tried to keep his father's sentiments in mind, but in the months that followed, it became easier and easier for Mark to forget that Kāʻeo was once his brother.

Not long after the funeral, Mark and Lana found an apartment in Kakaʻako. It was close to Mark's job and close to Mānoa, where Lana was enrolled. They signed the application, and three days later put down their deposit to hold the apartment. Ma didn't approve, but it didn't matter. Whenever she tried to remind Mark of the responsibility that he had to Kāʻeo, Mark would just think about how different his life would be once he was out of the house, and her voice would fade into the background. In contrast, Pops didn't bother to pressure Mark, and he didn't have to. Mark knew that his father expected more out of him, but as hard as Mark tried to, he just couldn't empathize with Pops' perspective. Kāʻeo had left. There was nothing more to it than that.

Shortly after he moved out, Mark's suspicions about what Kāʻeo was doing with Junior began to materialize: a run-in with a classmate at the drug store; a conversation with a neighbor at the mall; a random text message from a friend. All seemed innocent at first: *How's your brother doing? He still in school? Where's he's working now?* But there was always an underlying concern that made its way to the surface eventually: *I seen him by the Hygienic Store. He seemed real out of it. He's with Junior boy a lot, yah?* Mark kept the rumors to himself, but eventually the talk found its way to his parents anyway, the messages on their answering machine eating away at their memory of Kāʻeo. Through it all, Pops remained optimistic, encouraging Mark to do the same. But no longer at home, Mark had grown tired of his father's delusions, and although he did his best to humor his father, he knew that it was only a matter of time before things came to a head.

Mark was in his second month of freedom. He had stopped by the house to pick up the rest of his belongings. He found Pops in the kitchen, his father praying over a sink full of dishwater. "Sorry," Mark apologized, "I never mean fo interrupt."

"Not at all," Pops said, making the sign of the cross.

Mark noticed the glass rooster at the back of the sink. Pops had always been just as much Portuguese as he was Christian, believing in even the most bizarre of miracles, including stories of roosters intervening on behalf of dead men. *He wasn't dead yet*, Pops would always interject. "You really think dat going help?" Mark asked his father candidly.

"Can't hurt," Pops replied.

Mark kept his opinion to himself. "I jus get one more box, den I going go," he told his father.

Pops nodded. "I have something for you," Pops said. "Figured maybe if you have time." He walked past Mark and headed down the hall.

Mark followed Pops into his father's bedroom. "Wea Ma stay?" Mark asked, looking around. He walked over to his father's desk and noticed an open notebook near the phone, the cover folded back, messages scribbled in his father's shorthand.

"Out with Aunty Sheryl," Pops told him, walking over to his side of the bed to pick up a thin pamphlet. He offered it to Mark. "Ma's doing better, you know? She started seeing someone, it's been good for her," he added. "Good for all of us."

Mark had heard about the therapist from Elani, but his brother didn't offer much in the way of developments. "What is dis?" Mark said, opening the accordion fold. He read the headings: *Understanding Addiction*; *Tips for Parents and Families*; *Who to Call and Who Can Help.* "You got to be kidding me."

"Whatever is going on with your brother," Pops began. "You need to—"

"No," Mark said, quickly handing the pamphlet back to his father. "I no like hear how dis stay one disease or how he no can control what he doing. Dis Kā'eo, Pop, he get more brains than dat."

"It's easy to think that, Mark," Pops nodded. "But it's the exact opposite. Your brother, you know how he is, he has a way of holding things in, and it's those…" Pops said, picking up the pamphlet. He unfolded it out and read from one of the sections, "…emotional triggers that can play with his reasoning, and that's on top of…" Mark knew that his father still couldn't say it out loud. "And with Papa's history," Pops substituted.

"Why nobody else in dis family get one problem den, ah?"

"Listen," Pops held his hands up. "I just think…" Pops searched for the words. "I just wish you'd stop blaming him, Mark. I wish you'd just try and take a second to think about him, and what he's going through." Mark started to laugh, but Pops pressed forward. "And try to understand, you know, that maybe he needs our help, and that although we don't agree with what he's doing, we still have an obligation to try."

Mark looked at his father: Pops' eyes bloodshot, pools shaded deeply below them, and a thin layer of stubble gathered across his cheeks like dust. He recognized himself in that face. And even though it didn't seem possible, he recognized Tūtūpapa too. "You know, Pop," Mark began. "I dunno how many times I wen tell you sorry, you know, fo moving out, and I still sorry." Mark shook his head, "But no matter how many prayers you say, no matter how many excuses you make, none of dat going change what stay going on right down da road, you understand? What, you need fo catch him coming through da window fo believe?"

Pops shook his head. "He has an addiction, Mark," Pops finally said it. "He's not *the* addiction."

"He stay pathetic," Mark shot back. "He wen throw his whole life away, he wen throw his whole family away—"

"No," Pops interjected, "you're throwing your family away, Mark, don't you realize that?"

"I think you been hanging around da house too long, you know dat Pop?" Mark replied. "You starting fo sound like Ma."

"Maybe she's not as crazy as you think," Pops told him.

"Maybe," Mark said. "Try ask da therapist next time."

And that was how Mark left it with his father—divided on the topic—because that's what it had become for him: a topic to ignore, a topic to avoid, a topic to bury. Of course, the distance helped. Mark was no longer subject to his mother's fits or his father's lectures. His life was now filled with Friday night walks down to Ward for a movie or dinner; Saturday mornings at Ala Moana Beach Park; and Sundays spent having brunch at the Moana. But then there were moments that disturbed the calm, dredging his subconscious, bringing his anxieties up to the surface. Mark would wake up, his heart throttling against his chest, the same dream haunting him: Kāʻeo's body floating in a sea of debris, Mark watching the tide carry his brother further and further out, Pops' voice ringing in Mark's ears like a siren.

It was like that for months, unexpected, but always the same. Then one night Mark woke up, and the ringing wouldn't stop. Over and over he heard it, an incessant buzz that rattled the silence. "Mark," Lana slapped his head. "Mark, your phone."

Mark felt blindly for his cell. He looked at the display: It was 4 a.m. "Stay la—" before Mark could finish his sentence, his mother broke through, Ma rushing to speak between sobs. "Control yourself, Ma," Mark said, throwing the sheets to the side. "What?" he asked, her choking making her words indiscernible. "Wea Elani stay? Get Elani on da phone." All Mark could think about was Kāʻeo being carried off by the ocean.

"It's Pop," Elani's voice rushed through the speaker. "There was an accident."

Mark had to pause to catch his breath. "Wea he stay now?" Mark asked, searching the floor for something to throw on.

"Castle," Elani told him. "We're going there now."

Fuck. "Keh, I stay on my way," Mark hung up and got dressed.

"What's going on?" Lana asked him, still half asleep.

"My faddah," he told her. "He in da emergency room."

"What happened?"

Mark shook his head. He didn't know. "Stay hea, alright? I going call you."

"You sure?" she asked him.

Mark kissed her and picked up his keys. "I dunno what stay going on," Mark explained. "But whatever da fuck wen happen, I no think you like be dea." And he meant it.

By the time he got to the hospital, Pops was already in surgery. Ma was rocking in her seat, while Elani did his best to hold her still. "What da fuck wen happen?" Mark asked, trying to keep his voice down. A police officer was waiting to ask about what they had found at the scene.

"There were no signs of intoxication," the police officer said, moving down the report. "From the damage and the injuries, it looks like he fell asleep at the wheel." The police officer looked at the three of them, "Do you folks have any idea what he was doing out so late?"

Mark looked at Ma and then at Elani. "He was looking for our brother," Elani finally told the police officer, taking a breath. "He was looking for Kāʻeo," he said to Mark.

Mark left the emergency room in a daze. Pops had survived the surgery, but they weren't sure if he would wake up. "No disrespect," Mark said to the doctor, "but you no really sound hopeful." And she wasn't. They would do all they could for Pops, but in the meantime, they needed to let him rest. In the car, Mark tried to process what Elani had reported: that Pops had been searching for Kāʻeo. He skipped the Likelike and headed toward Kahaluʻu, driving along Kamehameha Highway. Just past the pier, Mark saw where his father had crashed: the guardrail pushed back, the tree just off the road hanging low.

That night, Mark had the dream again. Mark was on the shore, his brother drowning on the horizon, but this time, Pops was swimming out to meet him, struggling against the waves before slipping beneath them, too. Mark couldn't get back to sleep. He stayed up and stared at the ceiling, doing his best to keep the dream out of his mind.

"I jus no understand," Mark told Lana the next day. "Pops been out dea every night, fo what?" Mark shook his head. "Fo one good fo nutten who jus like get wasted and fuck around."

"That's your brother, Mark."

"You going give me dat shit too, ah?" Mark replied snidely.

Lana rolled her eyes at Mark. "You know," she began with caution, "the same thing could be said about us, about what we're doing."

"You mean about me?" Mark raised his eyebrows. "But you know what, last time I wen check, I been taking care of my responsibilities."

"I'm not—"

"No," Mark was adamant, "dis da same shit I been hearing all my life. Kāʻeo always wen give da orders, he always wen get da privileges, he always wen get da chance fo choose, but wen was my turn, nah. I stay da one dat need fo do double da work fo get half da credit. Bullshit, you know? And wen shit wen go sideways and Kāʻeo was in charge, Ma,

Pops, dey never wen look at him, dey always wen look at me, dey always wen ask what da fuck I wen do, or what I doing, so you know what? Fuck him. I get my life together, if Kāʻeo like waste his, das not my business." Mark got out of bed. "Unless dis badge goes gold," he said, holding up the silver security badge on his dresser. "Fuck him."

"You know, Mark," Lana began her lecture, but Mark cut her off before she could get any further than that.

"Jus never mind already, dis not your business anyway." He knew he would regret his words.

She bit her lip and exhaled through her nose. "Maybe you're right," she nodded. "Maybe it's not my business, but it's like I told you before, you need to seriously start thinking about what you're doing and why you're doing it," she said. "Because the choices that you're making, you're going to have to live with them, and as long as we're together, so am I."

Mark shook his head. "You stay so dramatic, you know dat?"

"You could do with taking things a bit more seriously for once in your life, Mark."

He leaned up against the dresser. "You no think I taking dis seriously?" Mark smacked his chest. "First Papa, now dis, and you no think I taking dis shit seriously." He shook his head at her. "And you know what, no ack li'dis was all my idea," Mark smirked. "You was da one who wanted fo move, too, so no put all dat on me."

"Well, maybe I was wrong," she admitted. "Maybe it was too soon. Maybe we should have waited until you had a chance to deal with everything at home first."

Mark could feel his neck heating up. "You know what, I going go," Mark told her, throwing on a shirt and shorts. "I need fo stop by da office and let my boss know what stay going on anyway, den I going go da hospital." He headed for the door. "I going see you tonight."

Lana stepped out into the hall. "You can't keep avoiding this, Mark," Lana told him, but he couldn't hear her with his heart pounding in his ears.

Before he went to the hospital, Mark stopped at his parents' house to rescue the glass rooster from its perch in the kitchen. All his life, Mark had heard Pops talk about the dollar-store knickknack with reverence, that as long as you had hope, there was a chance. It was waiting for Mark. Its beak broken, the paint worn from its chest down, but it was there. He held it in his hands, and for the first time, Mark said a prayer for his father.

When Mark got back in the car, he noticed that the low gas light was on. He drove over the bridge and pulled into the gas station. The only open pump was near the street, the Hygienic Store in clear view. Growing up in Kahaluʻu, Mark had grown accustomed to the stories: under the banyan tree, bodies gathered between parked cars, taking turns watching the road, making do with what they had. A strip of foil or a makeshift pipe, a broken light bulb, a straw, and then just a pinch in the end. Good enough for a couple of passes, good enough to get them through to the next pull. Maybe enough to keep them awake, to stop them from dreaming. To make them feel like they were flying, when really they were just drowning again.

The pump stopped with a jerk. He returned the nozzle and looked up, and that's when he saw it: Kāʻeo's truck pulling in to the stall next to his. But Kāʻeo wasn't behind the wheel. "Shit, Markie boy," Junior said, hopping out of the driver's seat, his sly grin pressing his red eyes into slits. "Fucking long time no see." He was skeleton thin, skin stretched taut across his cheekbones. His hair was cropped close to his scalp, bleached blonde and faded orange. He had a crystal in each ear.

"What da fuck?" Mark stood there, trying to make sense of what he was seeing. "Wea Kāʻeo stay?" He asked, falling back against his cab.

"Home," Junior said, the word rolling off his tongue with little weight. "Well, my place anyway. I tell you, dat fuckah, he no like leave fo nutten."

"What da fuck you doing wit his truck?" Mark sputtered, the words coming out just as shaky as he felt.

"I jus borrowing um fo now," Junior smiled again. "Why, you get one problem or something, Markie boy?"

Mark didn't know what to say or what to do. He looked at Kāʻeo's truck again, stunned. "Nah," he finally told him. "I jus, you know..." Mark didn't.

"Well I going see you around den, ah?" Junior said, throwing Mark another smirk. He was halfway to the door of the convenience when he turned around. "Oh, and Markie boy." Mark looked up. "No worry, I taking good care of your braddah, keh?" Junior said, leaving Mark to find his balance again.

Mark didn't wait until Junior got back. He got in his truck and started the engine. What else I going do? He thought, waiting to turn onto the main road, looking in his rearview mirror. Follow him, den what? Break down da door and drag Kāʻeo out, what if he not dea? What if he no like come? I not Papa, I not Pops, why he going listen to me? Mark wasn't his father, no. No, the best thing to do was to go. Fo go see Pops. To take care of the family that he could take care of. And then maybe when Pops was better, maybe den. *No worry, I taking good care of your braddah.* There was an opening. Mark took it, doing his best to put the encounter out of his mind.

Over the next week, Mark watched his father fall away organ by organ, until all that was left was a room full of machines and a decision to make, his decision to make, Ma's mind far from stable. He was sitting in the dark, holding Pops' hand, and wishing that Lana had come with him. But she had insisted on staying at her grandparents' house until Mark had dealt with things. Stay better this way: small, private, jus da family. He could hear the slow drip of the IV, the hum of the air conditioner, even the nurses down the hall, the soft squeak of their shoes as they moved across the tile. But his father was silent, his hands were cold, and every time Mark looked at him, he saw the wires snaking across the sheets and the emptiness in his face. His father's chest rose and then fell, moving up and down with each exhale of the breathing machine.

Mark lifted his father's union cap off his head and began to tame his father's curls over the shaved section of scalp, where the doctors had opened Pops' skull to stop the bleeding in his brain. If his father were awake, Pops would have stubbornly done it himself, taking the plastic comb he kept in his jeans and guiding the teeth as he had for years, but the accident had muted the humanity of habit. Now, the only things that remained were the machines, the blips and beeps posing as life. The white noise of their operations was a steady solace to the somber silence that Mark knew was only a matter of a few more signatures and forms.

By the time Mark had finished combing his father's hair, Elani was at the door, the hood of his sweatshirt dropped over his eyes. "Sorry, church got out late," Elani said. Ma appeared behind him, wearing a black cotton mu'umu'u with hala flowers made of orange thread, her gray hair hanging past her shoulders.

"Eh, stay alright, he jus wen tell me about dis new nurse, ah Pops? One pretty wahine," Mark slapped his father's knee, ignoring Pops' lack of response.

Ma stood in the doorway, looking at her husband. She approached him slowly, running her fingertips along his cheek, and then she pressed her lips to his skin and held them there, her left hand searching for a pulse. "You never reach him yet?" Ma asked Mark, removing her hands.

Mark wasn't expecting her to ask so soon, but he answered with little pause, the lie well rehearsed. "Kā'eo not hea, Ma, he busy," he said, as convincingly as possible.

"Too busy fo his faddah?" Ma looked at him with suspicion, searching his face. "You call him right now," she ordered. "Get him on da phone right now," she reached for the phone, nearly falling over.

Mark caught her, using his other hand to return the receiver to the cradle. "Ma, I told you already."

"I no care," she said, pushing Mark back. "He needs fo be hea today."

"We no can keep putting dis off, Ma," Mark told her.

But Ma's attention was on her husband again. "Oh, he was so handsome wit his beard full, shirt all unbuttoned. I never noticed anybody else," Ma's smile filled her whole face, her fingers running through her husband's hair. "Kā'eo get his nose, all you boys do."

"Ma," Mark touched the nape of her neck, a gesture that Pops always used to bring her back. "You need fo listen to me."

Ma's fingers lingered on her husband's hand. "Unless you going pick up dat phone right now, I no like hear anada word out your mouth, you understand?"

"I going get da nurse," Mark said, standing up. "See wen da doctor going come see us."

"You deaf or what?" Ma asked him.

"We hea fo make one plan, Ma. Da doctor going come explain things again, and I need fo sign couple papers. No more putting dis off." Mark paused, suddenly out of breath, "No more waiting, okay?"

Ma touched a hand to Pops', "Wen Kāʻeo come."

Mark sat down and pressed two fingers between his eyebrows, trying to relieve the pressure. "Ma," he started to plead.

"She has a point, you know," Elani interrupted from the corner. "You might not give a shit, but he has a say in this, too."

"Yah?" Mark shot a look at him. "Well let me know wen he like speak up, keh?"

"Shit needs to be said, that's all," Elani explained.

Mark looked at the both of them. "I not da one who wen decide dis, dis stay what Pops wanted us fo do jus in case da kine. He never like end up like Papa, suffering fo who knows how long."

"Give me his number then," Elani held out his hand. "You don't want to call him, I will."

"What I said already," Mark shook his head. "He stay busy, alright?"

"Bullshit," Elani challenged him. "Get him on the phone."

"Fo what? We no get da time or da money fo sit around and wait fo da prodigal son fo return, and I definitely no get da energy fo deal wit your fucking attitude right now." Mark didn't understand where his brother's aggression was coming from, "So, either sit da fuck down or shut da fuck up, keh?"

Elani got up and pulled his keys out of his pocket. "I'm not going to be here for this," he said, walking out the door. "I'm done." Mark didn't budge.

Ma stood straight up, her shoulders back, eyebrows furrowed. From where Mark sat, she looked like a moʻo towering over him. "Marcelo Kekoa Teixeira, Jr.," she began, "you jus going sit dea, huh? What you think your faddah would say, da two of you acking so disrespectful?"

"Ma—"

"Go," Ma ordered, not settling for anything less than compliance. Elani was almost to the elevator when Mark caught up to him.

"What da hell stay wrong wit you?" Mark called down the hall.

Elani pulled his hands out of his jacket. "Can't stand your shit, alright?" They stopped just short of the elevator. "I'm tired of your excuses and your whole fucking act."

Mark waited until a woman passed, and then lowered his voice. "What da fuck is your problem, Elani?"

"You," Elani said, concise and blunt. "Now, you give a shit. Now, you want to fucking come back and put shit back together? Fuck you." Mark grabbed Elani's jacket and shoved him up against the elevator door. "Get your hands off of me," Elani told him.

"I been hea every day, Elani. Every. Fucking. Day."

"Because you have to be."

"Cuz das our faddah in dea," Mark corrected Elani.

"You remember what you promised me, Mark?" Elani pushed Mark back. "Do you?"

"Dis not my fault," Mark brushed Elani off. "You like blame somebody, blame Kāʻeo."

"Like you do?" Elani asked, the question cutting Mark in the gut. "Why, because he was the oldest? Because you guys never got along?" Elani shook his head, "Grow up already."

"Cuz he never gave a shit about anything or anyone," Mark replied, his body shaking. "Cuz wen dis family wen need him, you know wea he was?"

"And where were you, Mark," Elani dug deeper, "when Pop needed you, huh? When he was out there looking for Kāʻeo, where were you?"

"I no need fo explain myself to you, you know dat?" Mark turned and started back down the hall.

"Did you talk to him? Did you call him or try to find out where he's at, at least?" Mark kept walking. "Did you?" Elani yelled, pressing the call button. "Do you even care?"

Mark turned to face him. "I no get time fo argue, keh? Pops stay dying in dea, I jus trying fo focus on da family dat still around."

"A little late," Elani told him. The elevator doors opened and Elani stepped inside. He hit the button for the lobby.

Mark stepped in after him. "He stay da one das supposed to be hea, you know dat? Fo talk Ma through dis, fo get Pops' shit in order, fo be da man of dis family, not me." Mark felt his eyes starting to burn, his body heating up. "Dis not what I wanted."

"Isn't it?" Elani brushed Mark's hand away. "He needs help, Mark, Pops knew that," Elani took his hood down and wiped his face. "You know that."

Mark thought about Junior, about their encounter at the gas station, how he had just stood there, helpless. "What I going do, huh? What I can do?"

The doors opened. Elani tucked his hands in his jacket pockets. "Whatever you have to," Elani said. "Whatever it takes." He turned around and headed for the hospital doors.

"Wea you going?" Mark asked, following close behind.

"Anywhere but here," Elani said, his attention elsewhere.

"What da fuck you talking about?" Mark asked him.

Elani didn't answer. "Find him," he finally said.

"Elani, I..."

"For Pop," Elani added, and then stepped out into the rain.

Mark stood there and watched Elani disappear in sheets of gray. Alone, he reached in his pocket for the glass rooster and turned it around in his hand, over and over again as he had for the past week. He thought about what Lana had told him, and about what Elani had said, and about their mother's pleas. Mark closed his eyes and he could see his father, praying at the sink. Mark ran his thumb over the beak and pressed down, thinking about what he had come to the hospital to do. Hope was gone and Mark had a choice to make, a choice that he had to live with, for his family and for himself.

Mark had spent the past week parked up the street from Junior's driveway, watching for his brother, under the cover of a large hau tree. He had seen Kāʻeo, or who he thought was his brother, more than once, his large body slumped in the back of his own truck, Junior in the driver's seat. Mark had borrowed Lana's car and followed them, waiting for the right opportunity to approach his brother, but the moment never presented itself: the two of them, often heading to Zippy's or the grocery store, or meeting up with others, some Mark recognized, but most were suspect to him.

On the one occasion that the possibility presented itself—Junior dropping Kāʻeo off outside a small house in Kailua—Mark had gone to the front door only to realize that his brother had gone around the back. He could hear two voices, what sounded like an argument between Kāʻeo and another man and then the distinct sound of fist on flesh, the other man screaming out in pain. Mark hid in the garage and waited, and a short time later, Kāʻeo came out with a DVD player and a small flat screen just in time for Junior to pull up to the curb. And that was when Mark realized that Pops had been wrong, Kāʻeo wasn't a victim, he was an accomplice. But for the sake of his father, Mark decided he had to remain vigilant, and so he continued to watch and to wait for his chance.

Before he picked up his mother for church, Mark woke up early and camped beside the same cluster of branches, trying to decide what his next move was going to be. With each day that passed, Pops' medical bills were rising, and Mark knew that they were out of time and out of options. Mark was going to have to act and soon.

A black Nissan truck passed Junior's house and pulled up next to Mark's truck, blocking him in. He had seen the truck go in and out of the driveway before, but had never seen who was in it, guessing that whoever it was had a vested interest in Junior's operation. Mark saw the driver's side door open. He checked to see if there was any way out, wishing that he had been paying better attention to the road. "What, you lost or something?" the driver asked, stepping up to the passenger side and resting his arms on the cab, his body taking up the entire window. This wasn't Junior's skeletal carcass but their voices carried the same lazy intonation. The man was built like he had spent most of his life beneath a hardhat, with veins like cables running up and over a body of concrete. He was older, somewhere closer to Pops' age, Mark guessed, large gold-rimmed bifocals contrasting his tawny hide.

But it was the man's left cheek that caught Mark's attention, his wiry beard unable to conceal the sinkhole drawing the skin toward its center. It was as if someone had carved out the space with a nail or a knife or a bullet. The man leaned in, giving Mark a chance to see the cicatrix, the umber flesh like a lump of spent resin. "You wen hear me or what?"

"Nah, nah," Mark responded, reaching for his keys, "jus cruising, uncle."

The man gave Mark a half-smile, amused. "I not your uncle," the man corrected Mark.

"Sorry, I stay waiting fo somebody…one friend of mine, we go da same church," Mark thought fast.

"Yah, who?" the man leaned in further.

Mark turned the engine. "No worries, alright, stay late already. Need fo pick up my maddah," Mark did his best to strengthen his appeal. "I going check my friend out later."

The man looked around before tapping his hand on the doorframe. "We no like trouble, das all," the man said. "You like trouble?" he smiled at Mark again, this time letting Mark see the full extent of his lips, the left side slightly twisted.

Mark put his hand on the stick. "No worry, unc—" Mark stopped himself. "I mean, no."

"Good," the man stepped away. "So, no let me catch you hanging around hea again, keh?" Mark nodded. "Look fo your friend somewea else," he added. The man got back in his truck and inched it far enough up to let Mark squeeze through. Mark moved fast but carefully, pulling off the grass and heading back to the highway. Before turning at the intersection, Mark looked over his shoulder: the truck in the same spot, guarding the road.

Mark dropped Ma off at her regular pew, and then left the church and went into the hall. His favorite part of mass was already waiting for him: pink bakery boxes set up on the counter top. Mark stretched out at a table, ate a cinnamon glaze, and looked at a disassembled Easter tableau on the stage, staring at the artificial savior and thinking of the obstacles in front of him. It wasn't just a matter of finding his brother and dealing with him, it was about dealing with whomever else he was with at the time. And if the man Mark had met that morning was there, Mark had no idea what he was going to do. It was another hurdle, another excuse for Mark to rethink his decision. Giving up wasn't an option, but it was one that Mark was close to considering. He thought of his father and what he would do.

Mark got up and left the hall, heading out to a set of repurposed houses, where the church hosted Sunday school and other community services. Near the back, Mark found the place that he was looking for: an open room, a circle of folding chairs situated in the center. Church hadn't gotten out yet, but the light was on.

A woman was on the opposite end of the space, setting up a table with refreshments: a jug of juice, a pitcher of water, and another pink bakery box. She turned when she heard Mark climb the stairs. "Come in," she told him. "Group doesn't start for another fifteen minutes, but help yourself to some food."

Mark had never attended any of the support meetings, but he knew that his father had. "Thanks," he said to the woman, and then wandered around the room.

"My name's Marietta," she told him, extending her hand.

"Matt," Mark said, reaching for hers.

"Matt, huh?" Marietta nodded, looking Mark over. "You know,

what goes on here, it doesn't leave the room."

Mark considered her appeal. "I mean, Mark," he admitted. They shook.

"I'm guessing, it's your first time," she said, finding a seat in the circle. She tapped the chair beside her, offering it to Mark.

He was quick to shoot down her assumption. "Nah, nah, I not one druggie," he told her, leaning against the wall. "I jus, you know, was checking dis place out."

"Two things," Marietta told him, holding up her fingers. "One, this group's for family and friends, we support each other, we care for each other, we don't judge each other, you understand?" Marietta continued, "Two, the same goes for whomever brought you here."

"I jus curious, das all, always wen walk by dis place," Mark backpedaled. "I stay waiting fo my maddah get out of church and—"

"You're here," Marietta finished his sentence, "and that's okay."

Mark crossed his arms, resisting her hospitality. "So what, you one counselor or something?"

Marietta shook her head. "I'm just a mom," she confessed. "Been working to help my daughter with her disease for about ten years now."

"Drugs, you mean," Mark corrected her.

She took note of Mark's perspective with a nod. "You know," she began. "I remember when I first found out about my daughter. I yelled at her and screamed, locked her in her room, took the keys to her car. I didn't kick her out, not yet anyway," Marietta remarked. "I was angry at her," she looked at Mark. "And the worse things got, the angrier I became. And any time she came around, I reminded her of how she was disappointing me. I worked my ass off to put her through private school, and she worked her ass off to get straight A's, she could have gotten into any college she wanted to."

"Sounds like one good kid," Mark commented.

"She was," Marietta said. "And she is, and it took me a long time for me to realize that, a lot of long nights, a lot of stressful ones, as I'm sure you know." Mark kept his face straight, taking her advice in but not willing to admit it. "If it was just drugs," Marietta added, "it would be easy, but it's more than that."

"Stay pretty simple to me," Mark told her, just like he had told

Pops. "Stay one problem dat needs fo be dealt wit, das all."

"It's not that simple either," Marietta explained. "It's like cancer, there are ways to treat it, but it's more complicated than just cutting it out."

Mark was still skeptical. "Nobody ever choose fo get cancer," Mark replied.

"Whoever said addiction was a choice?" Marietta asked him.

Mark stepped away from the wall. "So what, you and your daughter…"

"We're better now," Marietta told him. "Once I realized who I was really angry with."

"Her dealer?" Mark said the first thing that came to mind. "Sorry," he took it back.

Marietta got out of her seat and walked over a table near the refreshments, a collection of literature and pamphlets spread across the surface. When she returned, Marietta offered Mark the same pamphlet that Pops had offered him once before. "Take it," she told him. "It will help."

"Like I already wen tell you, I jus checking dis place out, das all," Mark said, leaving his hands at his sides. "I really no get one reason fo be hea."

"That's exactly why you should," she advised him, offering it to him again.

Out of respect, Mark took it from her, folding it and stuffing it in his pocket. He looked at the clock on the wall. "I got to go," Mark told her. "My maddah going—"

Marietta held up her hand to excuse him. "We're here every week," she said, letting him go.

When Mark got home, he spent his afternoon thinking about what Marietta had told him. Perhaps Mark had been too hard on Kāʻeo, perhaps he had put too much blame on his brother, but then what was Mark to make of Kāʻeo's actions now, of the work that Kāʻeo was doing for Junior, disease or not. Mark knew of other addicts: friends with friends or friends with family, and he had heard of break-ins and petty theft, tweakers cashing in on the equity of their relationships. But was there more to it than that: were those acts of free will or symptoms of the disease? What choice he really get? Mark thought, thinking about Junior behind the wheel of Kāʻeoʻs truck, and about the addiction eating away at his brotherʻs willpower. Mark was coming to realize the answer, but the realization wasnʻt as reassuring as he had hoped. It was an old fear coming back: Markʻs fear of finally confronting his brother, and with that, confronting his own selfishness and judgments.

Mark stopped pacing and walked over to the counter, where he had emptied his pockets. The pamphlet was there, nearly open, resisting the fold. He sat on the floor and read it like he should have done when his father first offered it to him. *Avoid self-blame. You cannot make your loved oneʻs decisions, and you cannot make them want to change.* But Mark had to try. Kāʻeo deserved a chance.

It was dark by the time Mark finally got back to Kahaluʻu. He was tired of waiting, tired of thinking, and tired of making excuses. He took out a metal bat from behind the driverʻs seat, testing its weight, the air whistling with each swing. Mark knew that it wouldnʻt be enough to put Junior and his goons down, but he wasnʻt planning for a fight. He just needed to get their attention.

Mark flew up the driveway and hopped the gate.

The dogs brought the floodlights to life, but he was already nearing the garage, his eyes locked on the windshield of Kāʻeoʻs truck. Junior was going to pay. Mark let go, whipping the bat down, the glass blossoming fissures that danced in the light. He went for the hood, then the headlights, and then the passenger side window. He heard tires creeping up behind him, crunching to a stop. He whipped around to meet Junior, ready to take his jaw next, but instead the man with the black Nissan got out of the cab, a spear gun aimed straight at Markʻs stomach.

"What da fuck you think you doing?" the man asked, Mark dropping the bat at his feet. "Das one start," he said, reaching for it. Junior appeared from behind him, his gaze veined with red coral. "You know dis fuckah, son?" the man asked, pointing at Mark with the spear gun.

Junior nodded. "What da fuck you wen do to my truck?" Junior pushed Mark hard. He picked up the bat and pressed the end to Mark's chest. "Huh?"

"What da fuck I told you," Junior's father yelled at Mark. "Now you come trespass on my property, you come damage my son's truck."

"Das not his," Mark replied. "Das my braddah's."

"Das not your business," Junior said, tapping the end of the bat up against Mark's chin.

Mark looked down the length of the bat, ready to call Junior's bluff. "I jus like talk wit my braddah."

Junior was quick, cutting hard into Mark's side. "I never give you permission fo speak," Junior said, showing off for his father. Once on the leg, twice on the back. Junior jammed the end into the fat beneath Mark's ribs, pinning him against the hood.

"I jus like my braddah, keh?" Mark wheezed. "Das all. I jus like talk wit Kāʻeo."

Junior hit Mark again. "What, you never hear of one fucking doorbell?" He hit him again. "You never try fo knock?"

Mark was on the ground now, the distinct taste of rust and dirt sticking to his gums. "Kāʻeo," Mark yelled with what little voice he had. "Kāʻeo, I need fo talk wit you."

Junior dropped the bat and wailed on Mark with his hands until his father pulled him away by the back of his tank top. Junior brushed his father off and crouched down, grabbing Mark's face. "You like me take you out fo one ride, Markie boy. You like me take you up Goat Hills and drop you in da fucking bushes?"

"Fuck you," Mark spit.

"Let him up," Junior's father pushed Junior back. "Up," he commanded Mark, flexing his left fist. "Dis how shit going go, keh? You seem like one good boy, one nice kid, like my boy hea, so I not going let him fucking lose you up da mountain, but I not going see you again either, yah? You going get lost and you going stay dat way, understand? You wen get two chances now, no fuck up again."

Mark fought through the pain and stood up straight, drunk with adrenaline. He smiled red and white. "Kāʻeo," he shouted. "Kāʻeo," he stepped forward, not backing down. "Kā—"

Junior's father grabbed Mark's throat and pinned him to the hood.

He applied pressure. Mark flailed for contact. "Strike three," he said, then took the bat from his son and cranked Mark's chest again.

    All Mark could hear was voices. He tried to get up but quickly fell back, his ribs screaming with pain. Each breath he took was an effort. He turned his head, struggling to open his eyes, the sockets swollen. Kāʻeo was stepping away from Junior and his father, backing up towards Mark, a pistol aimed at the both of them, Kāʻeo's hands shaking. Without taking the gun off of them, Kāʻeo picked Mark up, shouldering his weight. Mark found his footing, his knees shaking from the pain.

    "I going fucking kill you," Junior yelled after them. "You hear me, ʻeo? I going fucking kill you."

    Mark's head was spinning, his body in shock. He tried to focus, concentrating on putting one foot in front of the other. His truck was waiting for them. He pulled his keys out of his pocket and passed them to his brother. Kāʻeo opened the passenger side as quickly as he could and slid Mark inside. Mark watched Kāʻeo round the truck and get in the driver's seat. Kāʻeo opened the glove box and threw the gun inside. Mark took a breath, realizing that he had been holding it. He looked at Kāʻeo, taking his brother in for the first time in a year. He looked the same, thinner perhaps: his clothes draped on his body like they were a size too large, but it was Kāʻeo. The difference was best seen in the way his hands danced across the steering wheel, fidgeting with their placement or in the way his tongue continued to slide in and out of his mouth, tending the breaks. "Jus shut up," Kāʻeo told Mark before his brother could say a word. "Jus shut up and rest."

    They drove in silence: Kāʻeo focused on the road ahead. Mark barely holding on to consciousness. There were moments during their drive when Mark felt himself slipping away, when they would pull up to a stoplight and Mark would jerk forward, and the pain would just be too much. And then sometime after they made the turn at Windward City, Mark closed his eyes and he could see the ocean.

    They were kids again, on the beach at Kualoa. Kāʻeo was standing between Mark and the water. Mark was hunched over, ready to pounce.

"What I told you," Kāʻeo said. "Stay too rough alright."

"I know what I doing, I not you," Mark tempted Kāʻeo.

"I no care," Kāʻeo told him again. "You not going."

"Says who?" Mark looked over his shoulder, their parents and Tūtūpapa engrossed in story.

"You like me get Ma?" Kāʻeo was serious.

"Why, you no can handle? Need fo get Ma fight your battles fo you?" Mark slapped his stomach. He looked at Elani, his brother reading on the grass. "Eh, Elani, Kāʻeo like know if you get something fo him read, too."

"You keep playing around, Mark, I going show you."

"Show me what, huh?" Mark put his fists up and pumped his arms.

"No ack, Mark," Kāʻeo stepped forward, but Mark was too quick.

Mark kicked a spray of sand in Kāʻeo's face, and then socked him in the stomach. "Das right," Mark taunted Kāʻeo, standing over him. "Try stop me now, ah?" Mark ran into the water and started to swim as fast as he could. The water was rough, but it wasn't like it was his first time.

"You better watch out," Kāʻeo screamed. Mark could hear his brother behind him, cutting through the water with ease, but Mark had the lead and he intended to keep it.

When he got to Mokoliʻi, Mark quickly circled the island to the other side. But Kāʻeo was already there, climbing up the rocks. "How da fuck?"

Kāʻeo laughed, "Next time watch, keh? You might learn something."

"Fuck you," Mark shouted back, but Kāʻeo was in the water again, swimming out to touch the giant's toe. Mark tore after him, but before he could dive, he lost his footing and slipped on the rocks. A moment later, a wave bashed him against the reef.

Mark remembered the blood streaming in front of him, red surging up from his arm. He remembered gasping for air, but only taking in salt. He remembered closing his eyes and blacking out. But this time, his eyes remained open and he watched the light dance through the surface of the water. He saw Tūtūpapa dive down, but he also saw Kāʻeo thrashing back from the horizon and then diving to help pull him up.

Mark, he saw Kāʻeo mouth his name, bubbles escaping Kāʻeoʻs lips. "Mark," his brother said, shaking him. "Mark, come on."

Mark opened his eyes and then closed them, the fluorescent lights from the ceiling blinding him. He was in the emergency room: an IV hooked up to his arm, a plastic tag strapped to his wrist, his bed surrounded by curtains. Kāʻeo wasn't there.

He spent the day in the hospital. It could have been worse, a broken nose, a fractured jaw, and a few broken ribs. No internal bleeding. The fracture was minor, both his ribs and his jaw would heal on their own. The doctor gave him a prescription, two weeks off, and four more weeks of cautious optimism. Six weeks to sit and think about how close he had gotten, to death and to his brother. He called Lana to let her know what had happened and to ask her to pick him up. She was furious but would be right there.

But when Mark went outside to wait for her, he saw his truck and Kāʻeo, his brother smoking a cigarette on the edge of the truck bed. "I thought you wen…" Mark grappled with the words. "You been hea all morning?"

Kāʻeo nodded his head but didn't lift it. "I had fo…" Kāʻeo took a drag, his fingers pressed tight around the cigarette to keep it from shaking. "I jus had fo make sure you was okay."

"Kāʻeo, I," Mark began, wanting to apologize: fo not dragging your ass in dat one night; fo acting like you was one fucking ice head; fo not reaching out sooner. But "I dunno what fo say," was all that he could get out.

"I need one place fo stay or something," the words rushed out of Kāʻeoʻs mouth with the smoke. "I no can stick around hea, you understand? I no can…jus fo little while."

Mark and Lana had a couch that Kāʻeo could use, but Mark hesitated. You get one friend or something? Was what he was going to say, but then he realized his mistake. "Me and my girlfriend get one place in town."

"I no like…" Kāʻeo held up his hand.

"No," Mark insisted. "No worry about nutten."

Kāʻeo hopped down and put his cigarette out, and then looked up at Mark. "Why you was dea, huh?" Kāʻeo asked him. "Why you wen come fo talk wit me?"

Mark considered Kāʻeoʻs inquiry, Mark wondering if he should keep what had happened to Pops from Kāʻeo. The knowledge could make things worse for his brother, triggering Kāʻeoʻs addiction. But there was another possibility, a chance for Kāʻeo to see his disease for what it was, a cancer that was not only killing him but his family as well. "Try help me," Mark lifted his arm. "I need fo show you something," he said, and then the two of them went back into the hospital and made the long journey up to their father's room.

Sixty days, that's how long Mark had to wait to visit Kāʻeo. Sixty days after Mark had gotten out of the hospital. Sixty days after he had driven Kāʻeo to the clinic, his brother determined to find his way back. Mark bought a calendar from the front desk, thirteen months of photos of the staff and residents, of recovery, and hung it up on the kitchen wall. That first week, Mark didn't dare strike out a single day, nervous that the second he did, he would get the phone call telling him that Kāʻeo was gone. But then on Wednesday, he received a letter in his brother's hand: short and to the point. He was doing well: *Stay hard but stay good fo me be hea, fo be around people like me, people who stay doing better. People who like change.*

After the first letter home, the clinic insisted on a black out period: no correspondence in; no correspondence out. "Stay fo get him focused on wea he stay, you know?" Mark updated Ma and Elani. "Dey no like Kāʻeo get all da kine, can make him relapse, can make him get second thoughts."

"No make any sense," Ma was skeptical. "Dis really what stay best fo him, fo keep him from his family? What about his faddah?" The matter had yet to be settled.

"He needs fo figgah his life out, das what stay best fo him," Mark told her, knowing it was the truth. "And I been thinking, you know, Kāʻeo already wen say his goodbyes, I think stay best fo jus get everything over wit already and den wait fo have one da kine fo Pops. Not like we can afford one funeral right now anyway, ah?"

"I no like talk about dis today," Ma shook her head.

"Stay no reason fo wait around anymore, Ma," Mark reasoned with her. "We need fo jus move forward, yah, like Pops wen tell us fo do, like he wen want us fo do."

"So that's it then," Elani was still in shock, "we just get it over with and move on."

"Focus on sku, on your future," Mark advised his brother. "You get college fo think about, right? Decisions fo make? You no get time fo waste, Elani."

"It's not that easy," Elani said with the same candor, blunt and candid.

"I know dat," Mark calmly interjected, "but you know what, we need fo focus on da shit we can do, keh? Da shit we need fo do, jus like Kāʻeo stay doing. And yah, going be hard, ah, but you know what, need fo jus take things one week at one time, you understand? Cuz das da only way we going get through dis."

And that's how Mark took it, Monday to Sunday. Out on medical leave, Mark was able to help Ma with the paperwork at the hospital and to make the arrangements for Pops' body to be cremated. On Pops' final day, Mark had Father Dumadag give Pops his last rights, and then Mark waited with Ma until it was over, Elani leaving shortly after the machines were removed.

The transition to normalcy felt like a stop-motion daydream. Mark wasted his days on the couch, the hours passing empty in front of the TV, or in his truck, driving with no place to go, often circling the island before heading back to town. Nights were better, Lana there to distract him, but never for long. More than once, Mark woke up to check his phone, thinking that the hospital or his mother was calling. Twice, Mark swore that he heard someone pounding on the screen door of their apartment, but when he got up, it was only the wind and his negligence, the screen door rapping against the jamb. His nightmares continued, but when Mark woke up, the details of the dreams were fleeting like the impression left after a wave recedes from the sand.

"How long you think going be li'dis?" Mark had asked Lana one night. He was on his side, watching the reflection of the television set play across their window.

It took Lana a moment to answer him, sleep already having taken her more than once that evening. "I don't know," she mumbled.

"You think wen he gets out…?"

"You can't rely on that," she reminded him.

The thought scared him, but he knew just how likely a scenario it was. Mark had read the statistics: a 48% short-term success rate, 12% in the long-term, with most people relapsing after three years. He was scared for Kāʻeo, but more so for their family and for himself, and of the precarious nature of hope. Mark focused in on the reflection of the television screen, not even sure what he was watching anymore. "Jus need fo move forward, ah?"

"You've done everything you can for now," she reassured him, and she was right. It was enough to get him to close his eyes, to get him through to the morning. When Mark woke up, he drew a line through that first week, and made it a point to do so every day, no matter what. One week at one time, he kept telling himself. One week at one time.

The following Sunday, Mark began attending family meetings at the church. In the beginning, he chose to just sit and listen, introducing himself as "Mark" but sharing nothing more than that. And just as Marietta had told him before, the others did not pass judgment on Mark or on his reservation to speak; in fact, it was quite the opposite. After Mark introduced himself and sat, the group thanked him for his attendance and for his courage, and with each member who stood up and shared, Mark felt his discomfort begin to ease.

There were many stories that first day, but of all them, the one he remembered most was Mel's, another newcomer to the group. His daughter was an addict. Oxy, Vicodin, "it started when she tore one of the ligaments in her knee during practice." He smiled and talked about how his daughter had gone to UC Santa Cruz on a basketball scholarship, how time and time again, she had "literally" broken her body for the sport, but that this time it was different. Without the scholarship, they couldn't afford the tuition. She was back home, depressed, "and things only got worse from there."

Mel started talking about ice, about finding his daughter's pipe when he had gone to check in on her one night. "She had moved the mattress a half-inch from the wall," leaving a small stretch of box spring just big enough to go unnoticed, but she had used the trick before. He tried to "talk sense" into her but she didn't listen, so he kicked her out of the house, "and for the next couple of years I made excuses for why she wasn't around, until people started to talk and I couldn't lie about what she was doing anymore;" and then the excuses weren't about her, "they were about me: about why I couldn't help her; or why I needed to think about my other kids first; or why I needed to think about my career." Mel paused, the fingers on his right hand twitching and rubbing against each other, "I wasn't thinking about her, not really, and if I was, it was only to blame her for something that I wasn't doing," he admitted. "And now that she's in recovery," he feigned a smile and continued, "now that I realize the excuses I was making for myself, I guess I'm just trying to figure out what's next, and that's why I'm here." He thanked the group and then sat. Mark took a breath and clapped his hands.

After Mel spoke, Marietta reminded the group about the importance of working the steps. "Realizing that we only have the ability to change our own actions, that's an important part of it," Marietta began, looking at Mel and also at Mark. "That's what we're all here to do: to admit that we are powerless over the actions of our loved ones, to take an inventory of our own actions, and to begin to make the changes necessary for ourselves and for our loved one's recovery; and a large part of that is about being open and honest at every step, with ourselves and with others."

In preparation for the next meeting, Marietta asked each member of the group to reflect on the excuses that she or he had made, and why. So over the next week, Mark did just that, jotting down all of the things that he blamed on Kā'eo: the constant bickering and fights when they were kids, the lack of privilege and responsibility that Mark had always had to fight for, the tension between Mark and their mother, and the independence that he had yet to achieve. As he wrote, Mark found that much of his animosity toward Kā'eo had been more about his own insecurities and shortcomings. He blamed Kā'eo not because he deserved it, but because it was easier that way. It was a realization that brought an aspect of his nightmares to the surface, one that he had never thought about before: he had always remained on the shore, too selfish and too afraid to make a move of any kind, yet placing the fault on his brother.

"I guess I always wen feel like was him, but you know what?" he told Lana one morning over coffee. "I think dat was jus one excuse, you know, fo me not doing more, fo how afraid I was fo act: wit him, wit my family, wit you, you know?" The realization also gave him a sense of reassurance, that perhaps in some way he had never really been able to leave his brother behind. "Now, I think I jus need fo let all da bullshit go, yah? Need fo realize da shit I wen do and start fo do things different, better."

"And maybe not worry about making mistakes," Lana added.

"Das one part of dis, too, ah?" Mark replied. "Jus need fo do what I can, and fo do what I think stay best."

"You'll figure it out…we will," Lana told him, taking his hand. "You just need to keep trying."

Mark looked at her hand, at her ring finger. "Every day," he told her. "I promise you dat."

At the next meeting, Mark was reminded of Lana's advice. Another member, Nicole, talked about her mother's third relapse and about her struggle to hold her family together. "Stay like dis negotiation between your head and your heart. I like do what stay best fo her but I need fo think about what stay best fo my kids too, you know? I no like see their grandmaddah li'dat, das not safe, das not healthy. And I guess, I jus feel like every time I get one thing figured out, anada thing jus come up all kapakahi."

Other members were not allowed to crosstalk, but Mark couldn't help himself. "No give up, das all," Mark blurted out, before realizing his error. "Sorry," he apologized, but she didn't mind.

With each meeting and each week, Mark gained new insight and became more hopeful about the future. Following another member's advice, he started keeping a "Just for Today" list. On day thirty-five, his list read:

Tell my maddah I love her, and dat I stay proud wit how well she doing.

Tell Elani I stay stoked he going college, dat he going get in any sku he like, dat he stay da smartest fuckah I know.

Visit Pops, going talk wit him about how good things stay.

Thank Lana, tell her how happy she make me.

Pray fo Kāʻeo, fo him get better and come home.

Mark paused, the tip of his pen hovering above the notepad. *I not going be afraid,* he wrote. *I going forgive myself. I going move forward.*

Two weeks later, Mark and Lana packed a suitcase and a gym bag and headed out to Waikīkī, a celebration of their anniversary that was long overdue. They spent the afternoon getting settled, and the early evening mixing drinks and lying in bed. By the time they were hungry enough to leave their room, Mark was too tired to hit the strip, so they ordered room service and fell asleep to the sound of the ocean lapping at their window sill. And for the first time in a long time, Mark slept through the night.

The next morning at breakfast, Mark noticed a Japanese bride and groom being photographed on the beach by an entourage of planners and guests. He thought about Lana and about possibilities that for once over the last year felt viable and real. After the couple passed and the crowd cleared, he noticed a man on the beach, laughing with a group of friends, while just a few feet away, another man lay curled up in the sand, a collection of plastic bags at his feet. At a distance, they could have been related: their faces and their skin, all similar in shape and in tone.

"You okay?" Lana asked, sitting down at the table with her plate.

Mark nodded out of habit more than sincerity, but when he went to pick up his fork, he found his appetite had turned. "I think I like go home," Mark told her.

She looked at him over the lip of her coffee cup, confused. "You not feeling well?"

"I dunno."

"Something happen?"

"Nah," Mark shook his head. "I jus dunno what I stay doing hea, das all, no feel right."

"What'd you mean?" she asked him, taking a sip. "Everything was fine last night."

"I know dat," Mark replied quickly and then took a drink of water, finishing half his glass. He took a breath and finished the other half.

She stood up, "Maybe you need to lie down."

"No, no, sit down," Mark counted his breaths. "I stay okay," he told her, picking up his fork to keep up the deception.

"Something happened," she wasn't asking this time, "tell me."

"Nutten happened," Mark shook his head. "I jus…dis stay okay or what? Us being hea?" he asked her. "I mean, while he stay in dea."

Lana hesitated to answer, not because she didn't know how to respond, but because she needed the right words to do so. "Do you remember what you told me," Lana began, "after I asked you about the reservation, after I asked if you were sure?"

"Dat I wen get one good deal," he joked, not knowing what else to say.

"That you need to take time for yourself, that it's important for you, for us," Lana replied. "For Kāʻeo, too. You didn't want to feel like you put everything on hold again, like you were waiting around anymore, because you didn't want to put that on him."

Mark looked up at her and nodded, "I know dat," he said, "but—"

"You feel guilty?"

"I dunno."

"You haven't done anything wrong, Mark."

Mark looked over his shoulder; the man in the sand was alone now, his imagined brother gone. "Sitting hea, celebrating, enjoying all dis," Mark said, "no feel li'dat."

"Why, because you aren't in there with him?" Lana asked a moment later.

Mark hadn't considered that guilt, not consciously. "Maybe," he said, the thought rising to the surface now.

"That isn't on you," she said.

"I know dat."

"Like I've told you before, like you've told me, you've done everything you can for him, whatever happens next…" Lana stopped herself.

"I never cause da addiction, I no can control da addiction, I no can cure da addiction," Mark said the mantra that the group ended every meeting with. "But why he in dea, and I stay out hea, you know?" It was a question that he had since the first time he found out that Kāʻeo had been using and the one question that he had wished that he had asked Kāʻeo about. Now, every time Mark thought about it, he returned to the day after Tūtūpapa had died and to the night before his funeral. Choices, the ones you make and the ones that make you. Either way, Mark had realized that eventually you have to face both and the consequences that come with them. He could no longer keep his from his mind.

"You might never find out," Lana said honestly, "but are you going to let that hold you back?" Mark knew she was right.

That night, while Lana slept, Mark lay in bed and listened to the waves. Although his mind was on the days ahead, he thought past them: months, years. Him and Lana moving into a better place: a townhouse in ʻewa, decent rent, and central A/C. They would have enough left over to pay their bills and save for a mortgage. Maybe in a year, they would start the next step, a ring and a family. Three kids, the first two planned and the third one a surprise, and a dog. Mark wanted a masculine breed, Doberman or Pit, but he'd settle for a Chihuahua, brown fur with a marbling of white. He could see himself in a crowd with Lana and Ma, watching Elani in his cap and gown, bachelor's in hand, on his way to his master's. Mark closed his eyes and he could see Kāʻeo beside them, his presence faint but there; and then sleep passed over him, and Kāʻeo was gone.

Mark remembered the exact moment that he knew. It was the fifty-seventh day. The clinic had called to tell Mark that his visitation had been pushed back. During a "Mad Dog" session, the group had been venting their frustration, when Kāʻeo had asked to leave and go outside. "And what?" Mark asked. The counselor told him that the session wasn't over and that he needed to stay with the group, but Kāʻeo refused and threw a chair through one of the windows.

"We don't condone violence here," the nurse told Mark.

"I wen figgah he was doing good," Mark replied. "Why you guys never say something?"

"He functions out when he doesn't want to deal with things and stays outside by himself for long periods," she told him. "It's good that he finds ways to occupy his time and is reflecting, but he needs to work on what's inside, the real problems—and that's something that you can't help him with right now."

Mark understood, but he insisted. "So what den, what we looking at?"

She couldn't say, and it didn't matter. One week later, in the middle of a house meeting, Kāʻeo packed his things and left with no word as to where, though many attempted a guess. Mark considered camping outside Junior's, but even if Kāʻeo was there, Mark was in no condition to act.

The next day, Mark drove down to Kualoa Beach. He pulled his truck into the parking lot and sat there, looking out at Mokoliʻi and thinking about the last time he had talked with his brother. They were in Pops' hospital room, sitting side by side, the doors closed. The only light coming through was a slice of sun that came from between the curtains and fell across the two of them. "You ever like go back?" Kāʻeo asked without looking at Mark, his eyes searching the room. "Even fo jus change one thing," he said, biting his lip. "One more chance."

Mark nodded. "Plenny times," he replied, and he meant it. "Especially nowadays."

"Wen," Kāʻeo continued his inquiry. "Wen you like go back to?"

The list was long and the pain made it hard to speak. "Dat time I wen steal couple candies from Goodie Korner and wen blame um on you," Mark answered, bearing it anyway. "You?" he asked.

Kāʻeo turned to face his brother, to say what, Mark didn't know, but then Kāʻeo looked down at Mark's arm, at the scar that curved from out of Mark's sleeve and into the light. "Wen we was kids," Kāʻeo's tone changed, slowed. "Dat day you hit da reef."

"Was long time ago," Mark had strained a smile, surprised to hear Kāʻeo bring the topic up.

"No matter," Kāʻeo said, looking away again, fidgeting with the lining of the chair. "I sorry fo leaving you behind back den, fo not looking back soon enough."

"Not your fault," Mark told him. "I da one wen ack like one dipshit, you know, not listening to you."

"Eh, no can blame you fo dat," Kāʻeo said. Mark thought he meant it as a joke, but his brother wasn't smiling.

Mark thought about the gun Kāʻeo had been carrying, that he had thrown in the glove box, but more so about another item that belonged to his brother. Mark got up the courage, "Eh, can ask you something, you wen leave one set of keys in my truck," Mark started to describe them, but Kāʻeo interjected before Mark could finish, telling Mark about their grandfather's boat. "Maybe can come wit me fo check um out," Mark replied. "Can fix da fuckah up together."

"Maybe," Kāʻeo said. Mark detected the lack of confidence in his brother's voice. "Maybe not," Kāʻeo said softer.

"I going wait fo you," Mark assured him.

"You going be waiting one long time." Kāʻeo shook his head and looked at Mark: "Been waiting one long time."

"Das okay," Mark told his brother. "Get time, ah?"

"Some do," Kāʻeo said, and then turned to look at their father, "da rest of us no more."

"Get more time than you think" Mark had replied. "Jus need fo make da most of da time you get." Mark wasn't sure if his brother had understood what he was trying to tell him, or if Kāʻeo had even cared, but he had meant every word. "No waste um."

Mark opened the glove box. The gun was gone and so were the keys. Before Kāʻeo had checked himself in, he had asked to borrow Mark's truck. "I can take you," Mark insisted. They drove down to a storage yard in town. Kāʻeo had gone in with his backpack and returned without it. Considering their last encounter with Junior, Mark could guess why Kāʻeo had taken the gun, but the keys? Had it been only a few months before, Mark would have assumed that his brother would pawn the boat off, but now Mark preferred to think differently. He believed that Kāʻeo was more than the decisions that he had made; he knew that he was, and he trusted that eventually his brother would come to realize that too. He had to.

That Sunday—three days after Kāʻeo had left rehab, over two months after they had sat in their father's hospital room together, and almost a year after Mark had found Kāʻeo lying on the concrete outside of their family's home in Kahaluʻu—Mark stood up and shared his family's story with the group. When Mark was finished, he told them about Tūtūpapa's boat, and how he hoped to one day take it out with his brother. "I dunno if dat ever going happen, you know?" he confessed. "My girlfriend says I jus need fo be patient and trust dat things going be okay, and I know she stay right," he paused. "Stay hard," Mark admitted, "but dat no mean I going stop. Nah, das why I going keep my head up, ah?" he pressed his hand to the left side of his chest. "Fo me and my family, and das why I stay hea today," he added, hope beaten but breathing still.

Elani

Heaha ka puana o ka moe?

What is the answer to the dream?

Proverb 510, Pukui 6

With Kāʻeo's whereabouts unknown and Mark out of the house, Elani began to focus on his own future. As a fervent reader, he had always wanted to be a writer, but he always struggled with the mechanics of the discipline. The ideas came easy, and he had a running list of story drafts and failed starts: man-made labyrinths traversed by nameless heroes; post-apocalyptic landscapes littered with warring factions; and tribes battling imperial overlords across squandered lands. But it wasn't until he had read Ursula Le Guin's *The Dispossessed* in his junior year that he realized there was more to a good narrative than just premise and inspiration. It was then that he began to understand that books weren't hobby-craft spaceships, made-to-order and completed in an afternoon; no, they were ansibles, complicated communication devices transmitting across space and time, transcending both, and he wanted to construct his own, but how? That was what he hoped his future studies would teach him.

Elani was both practical and selective in his choice of schools, narrowing his list down to three: the University of Kansas, UC Riverside, and the University of Oregon. "Have you given any thought to UH?" Elani's counselor had asked him out of curiosity. "I'm not sure about science fiction, but I've heard that their English department is excellent."

Although Elani had heard similar comments about the distinction of the faculty and the courses that were offered there, the college didn't appeal to him. Unlike Kāʻeo, Elani had never had an interest in his surroundings, much less in writing about Hawaiʻi, a direction that he knew would be discussed and promoted at UH. Part of it was because

Elani felt confined by the conventions associated with literatures of Hawaiʻi: that is, plantation-era nostalgia and local sentiment, which Elani had gotten enough of from his grandfather's anecdotes and his English teacher's current curriculum. Another part was in the lack of connection that he felt to his culture. Elani just didn't see the value in studying the past and never had.

"I'm just looking to get away, you know?" Elani told his counselor, keeping him at a distance. "Experience something different, something new," he added, paraphrasing a poster on one of the walls: "Expand my horizons."

"Ah, the college experience," his counselor poked fun at the cliché, not realizing the irony on his walls.

"I'm just looking for more," Elani replied, and it was true. He wanted more than 227 miles of shoreline. He wanted a future that was boundless and open, "and I don't think I'm going to get it here."

"There's more opportunities at UH than you think, not to mention resident tuition rates," his counselor added, encouraging Elani to remain open-minded. "You could save even more if you decided to live at home while you go to school."

Home, it was the one current pulling him back. Elani thought about Tūtūpapa, made up and lifeless; about Kāʻeo, roaming the streets; and about Mark, half their room already in boxes. In his head, he could hear echoes of his parents' arguments: Ma's moods lunging and diving sharply, Pops doing his best to bear the weight. Over the last six months, his family had been drowning, and he didn't see that changing anytime soon. "I'll think about it," Elani said out of guilt more than obligation.

He spent the rest of his time with his counselor making plans and organizing a timetable. He had already started on his college applications but there was still the matter of how to pay for his tuition once he got in, a matter he was concerned with bringing up to his parents. When he got home, Elani found Pops at his desk again: a stack of open envelopes in front of him and a legal pad beside him. Pops threw a glance at Elani and then finished his calculation, one side of the page clearly not adding up to the other. "Do you need something?" Pops asked him.

Elani knew where the conversation would go even before it began. "Nah," Elani shook his head, "just wanted to see how you're doing."

"You'd be surprised how much a funeral costs, not to mention your mother's therapy…" Pops stopped himself, sparing his son. "How'd your meeting with the counselor go?" he inquired, changing the subject.

"Great, he thinks I might be able to get a full ride," Elani exaggerated the details for his father's sake. Although there was still a large selection of scholarships available, many of the deadlines had already passed. Worse case scenario, there was always student loans. A Pell Grant was possible, but financial servitude was more than likely.

Regardless, Elani was glad to see his father's shoulders drop. "You've got the grades," Pops assured him, squeezing Elani's arm. "You just let us know if you need anything, alright? We're here for you."

Elani appreciated the attempt. "Don't worry about it, okay Pop, I got this," Elani told him before he left, knowing that as soon as he was out of sight, his father would add another line of expenses to his list. When Elani got to his room, he lay belly down on his bed and stared at the pamphlet that his counselor had given him, tossing it to the floor without even bothering to skim through it. It didn't matter either way. He couldn't afford to leave.

With his college applications in the mail and his scholarship applications completed, the only thing left for Elani to do was wait. But as the days stretched on, and Mark's theories about Kāʻeo became more than speculation, the more conflicted Elani felt about his desire to get away. Late at night, Elani would wake up to hear Ma in the hallway, pacing back and forth, or in Kāʻeo's room, vacuuming the carpet. "Jus in case," she would tell Pops when he found her out of bed. On the nights that her anxiety got the best of her and she refused to follow him back to their bedroom, Pops would take her into the kitchen, make her something to drink, and plead for her to take one of the pills her psychiatrist had prescribed. The bargaining could last hours. Elani blocked the space between the door and the floor with a towel to keep the light out and started to sleep with one pillow over his head to muffle the sound, but it was never enough; and as her compulsions became more routine, Elani found himself delaying sleep to ensure that he would be able to get through to the morning. He did his best to keep his mind off of what was going on outside his door, distracting himself by studying for school or taking in a few chapters of a book. On the rare occasion that Elani saw Mark, Elani brought up the topic with little result. "Pops knows what stay going on," was his typical excuse. "You need fo jus trust him."

But Elani's concern was growing by the day, not just about their mother but about their father too. Rather than going back to bed after giving Ma her medicine, Pops started to leave the house, not coming home until it was time for him to get ready for work, chasing his coffee with the NoDoz that he kept in his pocket. When Elani tried to talk with his father about what was going on, Pops would ignore his questions and assure him that everything was fine. "She's seeing someone," he told Elani one night after a late dinner. Ma had already gone to shower and get ready for bed. "She's making progress," he said.

"What about you?" Elani asked, taking note of the bloodstones that were set in his father's face.

"I'm fine," Pops brushed off Elani's concern. "Just busy, that's all, you know how things are."

"Is there anything I can do?" Elani asked, considering the possible reasons for his father's late night outings. "I can do the grocery shopping if you want, you know, after school"—it was a wild guess—"or if you need me to pick up Ma's prescription at night"—a more logical motive.

Pops caught on to Elani's line of questioning, "Sometimes, I just want to go for a drive, you know? Clear my head." It was a legitimate excuse, but Elani suspected that there was more to it than that.

"You're not drinking right?" Elani asked even though it was an unlikely scenario. After Tūtūpapa's funeral, Pops had made it a point to purge the house of any and all alcohol. "I mean, if you are, it's dangerous for you to be—"

"No," Pops shot down his concern. "It's nothing like that, okay?"

The phone rang. Elani noticed the light blinking on the machine. He couldn't remember the last time he had seen it off. "I got it," Elani said, reaching for the phone, but his father was quicker.

"Probably just a telemarketer," Pops assured Elani. "I'm sure you've got school work to do," he threw in, before pressing the handset to his ear. When Elani got to his room, he stood in the doorway and listened. He couldn't make out more than a few words, but before his father hung up, Elani heard him confirm a time: "No, it's no problem. Okay, ten o'clock, I'll see you then."

Pops gave Ma her pill early that night and then settled in at his desk. At nine-thirty, Elani told Pops that he was going to the movies with a few of his friends. It was a rare occasion, but his father was too busy with his paperwork to raise an inquiry. "You need gas money?" Pops asked him. His friend was going to pick him up at the bus stop down the road. "Be safe," Pops raised his head and gave Elani a smile.

"You too," Elani told him and then left.

Outside, Elani played it safe. He had thought of following Pops, but in Tūtūpapa's station wagon, he knew that he would be easily made. Instead, Elani headed down the sidewalk and waited on his neighbor's rock wall until the garage light went off, and then snuck back to the driveway and into the camper on his father's pickup, using the spare key that he found on top of the refrigerator to unlock the latch. When he heard footsteps outside, Elani held still, not even bothering to press his body out of sight. He stayed motionless until Pops backed out of the garage and headed down the road.

Elani paid attention to his surroundings, tracking his father's path by the lights and foliage that passed overhead, occasionally raising his head to confirm where they were. It was a short trip down Kahekili Highway: past the fluorescent theater sign, through the dip and its low-hanging trees, and a left turn onto Ha'ikū 's orange-bulbed neighborhoods. When Pops finally parked, Elani recognized the red neon hue of the Zippy's logo above him.

After his father had gone inside, Elani got out to see what Pops was up to. Through the window, he could see his father at one of the tables. A man joined Pops, and Elani recognized his face: he was one of his father's friends from church, from the meetings that Pops had been attending. Elani laughed at how stupid he had been. What the fuck now? he thought, realizing that he had no other choice. He stretched his legs and settled back in, anxious to get to his bed and get some sleep.

But his night was far from over. Rather than head back up Ha'ikū, Pops took a right onto Kamehameha Highway, and from there began to troll the stretch: shopping centers closed for the night, 24-hour grocery stores, karaoke bars. When Elani smelled the wet stink of harbor water, he lifted his head and saw the pier and he was hopeful that they were heading home. But his father continued on, this time drifting along the back roads, winding down thresholds of infrequent darkness. Once, the truck slowed to a stop and remained idle. Elani heard his father roll his window down, but Pops remained silent. By the time Elani looked to find out what his father had seen, the truck had started moving again, and all Elani could make out was the shape of a person, or was it something else, he couldn't be sure.

When they finally got home, it was well after midnight. Elani lay in bed, the afterimage from the streetlights keeping him awake. He remembered the night before Tūtūpapa's funeral. He had waited until he had seen the hall light go off before sneaking into the living room to investigate what his father had been up to outside. When Elani saw Kāʻeo slumped in his chair, a ripple of familiarity came over him: his brother's limp body reminding Elani of their grandfather's. It was the last time that Elani had seen his brother, and he realized now that it had probably been the last time that Pops had spoken with Kāʻeo.

What had prompted Pops to stop that night didn't matter. Elani knew what his father had expected to find, and perhaps it was better that it was a stranger, or a shadow, or a ghost—a relief that it wasn't Kāʻeo on the side of the road. Or perhaps it was worse, a reason for his father to continue his search, but for how long? When would it stop? He wasn't sure that he wanted to be there to find out.

The night that the police had found Pops' truck wrapped around a tree on Kamehameha Highway, Elani had been looking over class listings at the University of Oregon. Even though Kansas was his first choice, he felt that Oregon's program offered him a more diverse course of study, and although not as affordable as Kansas, was certainly cheaper than Riverside. Mānoa was the best choice in that regard, but Elani knew that if he stayed, it was only a matter of time before he too was consumed.

Outside of the emergency room, Elani told Mark about their father's nightly searches. Mark rationalized other theories. "You dunno,"

Mark said. "Prolly was jus driving fo get away from everything, fo get some time to himself."

"You don't know how bad it is," Elani replied. "I tried to tell you but—"

"You dunno what da fuck you talking about," Mark shook him off.

"I was there, Mark," Elani said. "You haven't seen him like this."

"Pops stay smarter than dat."

"Think, Mark," Elani urged him. "I told you how shit was with Ma, you think it's been any better now?"

"Everything was under control," Mark started pacing back and forth across the walkway. "Everything was good."

Elani watched his brother move from one side to the other. "For you maybe," Elani said, realizing just how long it had been since he had seen Mark in person.

Mark snapped out of his head. "Dis stay his fault, you know dat?" Mark spit on the ground. "All dis cuz of him."

Elani was used to his brother's hostility toward Kāʻeo, and he didn't want to hear it, not right now. Not with Pops' head being pieced back together on the other side of the sliding door. "Think what you want," he told Mark, throwing a look at Ma through the glass. "I'm going back inside."

"He's one tweaker, Elani, one ice head."

Does it matter? Elani wanted to turn around and tell Mark, but Elani didn't care to hear his brother's response and he didn't need to. Mark had made it clear where he stood the moment that he had moved out.

The night after it happened, Elani put Ma to bed and drove out to the spot where Pops had crashed. The houses that lined the left side of the road trailed red and green when he passed: Christmas specters that eventually gave way to the ocean, to branches that hung like phantoms, crackling shades in the salted breeze. There was no sidewalk, only gravel and dirt. Branches hung low and a hand-painted *Slow Down* sign leaned crooked on one side of the street. Elani felt the skin on the back of his neck rise.

And then he saw it, the skid marks on the asphalt, the guardrail bent out toward the water. Elani parked his car in the grass on the opposite side and got out. The tree Pops had hit was broken at the center, its branches dipping down to meet the ocean. Elani could make out fragments of Pops' windshield glimmering in the dirt, a few large chunks scattered across the ground like pieces of his father's skull. Elani looked over the ledge and saw a flash of white between the rocks. He got on his knees and reached down, pulling up the union cap that Pops always kept on his dashboard.

Elani sat in the dirt and cried.

When Mark called to tell him that he was with Kā'eo, Elani had already given up on staying. It wasn't just Pops' accident or the events of the year before. It was about what was next, or rather who. For one of his final assignments of his senior year, Elani was tasked with answering the question: "Who am I?" While his classmates wrote about their cultural heritage or about their upbringing or about their childhood, Elani wrote about what was left of his family. He was supposed to end the essay with a series of open-ended questions, and so he did: *Death, tragedy, addiction, is this what has come to define me? Is this who I am?* Although he had never written it down, the answer had been haunting him. He had already received acceptance letters from three of the four universities he had applied to, but only one, UH, had offered him the money that he needed. It didn't matter. He had made his decision and he was willing to make the necessary sacrifices for it.

At first, Elani didn't realize what his brother was telling him. "We jus wen get back from da hospital," Mark told Elani over the phone. "He stay at my place right now." He stood there holding the phone, his tongue heavy and dry. "Elani, you stay dea or what?" his brother asked.

"Yeah," Elani said, walking over to the sink to make a glass of water. "But I don't understand, where did you find him? How?"

"Dat shit no matter right now, he stay done wit all dat," Mark told him. "We wen talk, he wen see Pop. He stay ready, Elani."

Elani took a large gulp from his glass. "For what?" he asked.

"You so Pordagee, you know dat?" Mark joked. "I going take him down da clinic dis afternoon, check him in, make sure everything go good."

Elani wasn't sure what to say. He noticed the circle of hard water where their father's glass rooster had always been. He thought of his father's hat between the rocks. "And then what?"

"Shit going change, Elani. Kāʻeo going get better."

Like Papa? Like Pops? Elani wanted to say, but he held his grief in. Bullshit, he thought, denying the news. "Bring him here," Elani challenged Mark, wanting to see their brother for himself.

"I wen try dat already, he no like see nobody yet," Mark replied.

"Let me talk to him then."

"He stay sleeping right now," Mark replied. "We wen have one long night."

"And then what?" Elani blurted out.

"Why da fuck you keep asking dat, Elani?" Mark asked, his frustration apparent in his tone. "What da fuck you want me fo say?"

He didn't know. "I got to go," Elani told him.

"Let me talk to Ma," Mark said.

In the kitchen window, Elani could see his face stretched and divided by the jalousies. "I'll have her call you back," he said, and then hung up the phone.

Over the next week, Elani tried not to think about what was next. When Mark came over to give Ma and him an update on Kāʻeo, Elani just sat there, numb to Mark's forecast. *Focus on sku,* Mark had said, *on your future.* "It's not that easy," he had told Mark, and he had meant it. Although he had already signed his acceptance letter to Oregon, he had yet to send it. Can I really leave now? It was a question that he kept asking himself.

By the time it came to take Pops off of life support, Elani thought that he would have his mind made up. He stood and watched the machines being turned off, and thought about what Pops had said when he had first brought the possibility up to his father, *Whatever you decide, you got to do what you think's right for you.* But he knew that his father didn't believe that. No, when family no take care, you take care. Elani knew that was what Pops must have been thinking, but he had always been the selfless one. The breathing tube was removed and Pops started to heave dry gasps of air. Ma cried. Even in his current state, Mark held her. But Mark had already made his mistakes and paid for them, he had taken his chance. What if Mark wasn't there? Elani thought, could he make the call to kill their father or to nearly die going after Kāʻeo? How much help could I really be? Pops' eyes opened and Elani felt his stomach turn. He walked out of the room and down the hall, puking into an open trash bin, and stayed there, spitting saliva until Mark and Ma came out of the room.

For over two months, Elani grappled with his conscience. His family needed him. Kāʻeo needed him. It was the right thing to do, but when Mark told Ma and him that their brother had abandoned the program, Elani suddenly knew that it wasn't a matter of right or wrong.

"I wen go down dea today," Mark told them in the living room. "His therapist said he was doing good, but he never like da way things was being done. She thinks he going try anada program."

Elani was sitting in the corner of the couch, arms crossed. He had stopped listening. "What's the difference?" Elani asked.

Mark continued, misunderstanding his brother. "Guess da place stay like occupational-therapy," Mark explained. "I wen call dem today, but dey never like tell me nutten. I going try stop by later on."

"That's not what I meant," Elani said. "I mean what does it matter if he went to another program or he fucking went down the road, we all know what's going to happen in the end, right?"

"Eh," Mark threw a look at their mother, who was already on the verge of tears, and then turned back to Elani. "Dat kine not going help nobody, you know? Like I wen tell you before, dis not going be easy, but we need fo stay positive and jus—"

"You should talk, you know that," Elani interrupted. "You know how long we had to listen to you act like Kāʻeo was some fucking junkie piece of shit."

"You know, Elani," Mark began, "I get dat shit been hard fo you, but shit stay hard fo everybody right now, keh? Das how dis goes, we no can control Kāʻeo, you understand? Or what he like do wit himself."

"Bet it's easier when you don't have to live with it, right?" Elani threw at him.

"Elani Anthony Teixeira, you need fo calm down and listen to your braddah," Ma advised Elani, wiping her eyes with the collar of her blouse. "I no like hear anymore disrespect."

"I no like do dis," Mark said, doing his best to defuse the situation. "Come on, Ma," Mark walked over to her and took her arm. "I going take you fo eat, get your mind off all dis," he told her, walking her to the door. "You welcome fo join us, if you like," Mark said to Elani. "Or can stay hea and cool down."

Elani got up and started toward his room. "Nah, I don't want to live in your fantasy," he shot back. "Try to make sure she's in the house before you scurry back to town."

Mark left Ma at the door and went after Elani. "You stay fucking wit me or what, huh? We was done wit dis."

"You know," Elani began throwing open his door. "When you first told me that he was going to be in treatment, I didn't know what to say, yeah? I just thought, fuck, is this really happening or what? And I wanted to just write the whole thing off, just like you did before, but I believed the shit you said, you know that? That he was going to get better, that he was really going to change. I fucking believed you."

"Dis not li'dat," Mark replied. "Kāʻeo get one disease, Elani, and not da kine get one cure, you know?"

"Exactly," Elani turned around. "So stop acting like shit's going to change. No matter what happens, he's going to end up dead, and I don't want to be here when he does, alright?"

"So das how you going be den?" Mark asked. "You jus going give up, ack like you no give a shit?"

"Nah," Elani said, reaching for the envelope on his dresser. "I'm going to do what you told me to do," he added, showing his brother the address. "What Pop told me to do. I'm going to think about my future, I'm going to do what's right for myself and I don't give a shit what you have to say about it."

"You need fo jus stop, keh?" Mark put his hands up, blocking Elani's way. "Think about what you saying right now."

Elani pressed his chest against his brother's. "I have," he said, "and I'm done, just like you were when you left."

Mark held his position. "You think was easy fo me, ah? You think I wen move out and was like one fantasy, like me and Lana was jus sipping cocktails and fucking cruising, but I going tell you dis, was never one week I never wen wake up and hate myself fo leaving you, and Pops, and Ma. Was never one week I never think about Kāʻeo."

"Yeah, and it never changed shit, did it?"

"Stay easy fo ack like you no care, Elani, but shit going eat away at you, you understand? And one year from now, you no like be how I was, hating myself fo all da time I wen waste, fo treating Kāʻeo like he was one problem I never like deal wit."

"That's where you're wrong," Elani told him. "I've been here, I've dealt with this already."

"No," Mark pushed back, "you jus been hiding in your room, waiting fo somebody else make things right. Stay time fo you make dat change."

Elani just stared at Mark, unable to refute his accusation. "Get the fuck out of my way," Elani demanded. "I don't have time for your bullshit. I have things I need to do."

Mark stepped to the side. He couldn't force his brother to see his point. "You sure you want dis, Elani?" Mark asked him.

From where Elani stood, he had a clear view of their brother's room. After Kāʻeo had gone into treatment, Ma had opened it up to let the sunlight in and the stagnant air out in preparation for his return, but he could still smell the stale heat. In his mind, Elani could still hear his mother's nightly compulsions, and the endless whir of the vacuum's motor. He could still make out Pops' whispers, and the sound of their footsteps as he led her down the hall. Elani was still in the back of their father's pick-up, dredging the darkness for Kāʻeo's body, knowing what he would find.

When Elani first arrived in Oregon, he felt a sense of relief but also an undercurrent of dread, his brother's warning still fresh in his mind. It was reassuring to know that Mark and Lana had moved back home to take care of Ma, and that even though no one had heard from Kāʻeo since he had left treatment, Mark had not given up. Elani on the other hand did his best not to think of where their brother was or what he was doing; he couldn't, not after Tūtūpapa, not after Pops. Instead, he focused on the life in front of him and denied the one that he had left behind, determined to move on.

It helped to be elsewhere. Elani's acclimation to his new home provided a necessary distraction. At school, Elani went by his middle name, Anthony, which his roommate Jeff shortened to Tony to mark Elani's "successful emigration to the States." Elani was indifferent to the moniker. It had the benefit of being easier for his classmates and his professors to pronounce, and thus easier for him to assimilate effectively. In class, Tony was contemplative and engaged. He asked questions and spoke up, often beginning the discussion or closing it out strong. Outside of class, Tony socialized for the sake of the experience, feigning charisma and confidence, but like he always had, Elani devoted most of his free time to his studies. He preferred it that way. And so for the first two months that he was there, he was able to maintain a balanced trajectory, and then news of Kāʻeo's whereabouts surfaced and he was thrown off course.

It was a Friday night, the first week of October, Elani was lying in bed, annotating a story for his Intro to Fiction class, when he saw Mark's number flash across his phone's display. He silenced the call and waited for it to go to voicemail. The display lit up again. "I'm kind of busy right now," Elani finally answered, holding the phone loosely to his ear.

"Das what you always tell me, but den you never call back," Mark pointed out.

"Well, what'd you expect, Mark, I have a lot going on here," he rationalized.

"Das right, you always stay working on one paper, or studying fo one test, or going fo meet somebody—since wen you stay so sociable?"

"Is this why you called me? To lecture me on phone etiquette because I really don't—"

"Nah," Mark fell back. "I jus wanted fo let you know, I been checking in wit da programs and da shelters downtown. Dis one place told me one guy named Kāʻeo was in and out of dea couple months ago, I going check um out tomorrow." Elani put down his pen but remained silent, not sure of what to say. "I get one good feeling about dis, Elani," Mark made his appeal.

"Yeah," was Elani's only response, he had heard the story before.

"Da lady at da shelter said he wen look clean, sober. Dat he always wen try fo help out wen he was staying dea."

"I got to go," Elani picked up his pen again and stared at his textbook. "I'll talk to you later."

"Eh, Elani," Mark spit out before Elani could hang up. "We stay proud of what you doing, but we miss you, too, you know? Stay so long since Ma wen hear from you, she confuse you wit da Lau kid next door," he joked. Elani didn't care to humor his brother. He flipped his cell phone closed and got back to work.

Unfortunately, every time Elani read a sentence or skimmed a paragraph, he thought about what his brother had said. Clean? If it was true, then why wasn't Kāʻeo at home, why would he be holed up on a cot in a corner of some lice nest when Ma probably had his sheets washed and his bed made up, his room probably cleaner than any other space in the house. Sober? Elani thought about the time that Tūtūpapa had spent in Kāʻeo's room while he was in treatment. He thought about hearing Tūtūpapa get up in the middle of the night and walk into the kitchen. Elani remembered catching him once, his grandfather's hands shakily probing the pantry shelves and refrigerator drawers, and then eyeing the car keys hanging from the hook. It was those moments that shook Elani the most. The ones that reminded him that addiction is a rip current, unpredictable and recurring. Elani could see the exhaustion on his grandfather's face that night. The thought of it made Elani's eyes blur and his mouth dry.

Midway through his third reading, Jeff burst into their dorm room, nodding to an invisible bass line. Normally, Elani would disregard his roommate and continue on with his assignment, but after Mark's phone call, Elani doubted he was going to get much of anything done that night. "What are you up to?" Elani asked Jeff, watching him pick through the piles of dirty laundry on his side of the room.

Jeff raised his head and one of his eyebrows. "Going out," Jeff brushed Elani's inquiry off, knowing Elani's opinion of his antics.

"I figured that, dipshit, where?" Elani pushed. He could use a change of scenery to clear his head.

"It almost sounds like you're interested, Tony," Jeff brought the beat over to Elani. "Is that what I'm hearing or what?" Jeff picked the textbook up and out of Elani's hands. "You actually want to come up for air?"

"I don't want to get into anything stupid," Elani replied, having known Jeff to waste his nights hurling piss balloons out of car windows and stealing window clings from the McDonald's in town.

Jeff stood proudly in front of the Egg McMuffin poster tacked to his wall. "Hey, you're only dumb once," he remarked, offering Elani little to assuage his worries, but if Elani was honest with himself, he really didn't care.

They ended up at a house near Mission City Park. The door was unlocked, and the walls were humming. Jeff ushered him through the noise and into the living room, where he picked up two shot glasses and handed one to Elani. "Don't give me that look, Tony," Jeff shouted over the incessant thump of EDM. "This is why you're here, right?" Elani knew that hesitation was pointless; he had already come this far. He knocked the shot back without thinking. The tequila burned all the way down. "That's what I'm talking about," his roommate hollered. Jeff grabbed the bottle off of the table and poured them both another round.

From that point on, the night was charged and every time Elani threw back a glass or a bottle or a cup, he could feel the lightning surge in his stomach. Everything around him was laughter and electricity, an ambient field of bass and synths, booming and squealing. He bounced from room to room, body to body, losing himself to the current, until a jolt hit him and the lights suddenly went out.

Elani was in the air but he wasn't. The cabin was dim, the emergency lights pulsing. He felt a hand on his shoulder. Tūtūpapa was dead beside him, his body floating out of his seat. Elani opened his mouth to scream but swallowed water instead. He unbuckled his seat belt and went for the door. It held tight. There was no escape.

When Elani finally came to, there was a woman standing over him. He was covered in sweat and his heartbeat was erratic. "Are you okay?" she asked him. From the urgency in her voice, Elani could tell that it wasn't the first time that she had asked. He blinked until his eyes adjusted and then looked around. No plane, no Tūtūpapa, no water. He was in the backyard, lying in the grass. The party had died down but he could still hear the music throbbing with his forehead, a sound reminder of where he was.

"What the hell happened?" Elani mumbled over the bass.

"I was looking for my sister and found you out here," she said. "Is your head okay?" She reached around and pressed her fingers over Elani's scalp.

"I'm fine," he told her, his elbows buckling when he attempted to stand.

"Let me help you," she said, reaching under his arm and pulling him up.

Elani dusted the grass off of his jeans and threw a glance at her. Her hair was pulled back and he could make out the soft outline of her face in the light, her lips naked, a strand of flowers inked behind her earlobe. He quickly turned away, heat blushing over his cheeks. "I'm such an idiot," he shook his head at his lack of self-control.

"You had a little too much, that's all," she told him.

"I know better, believe me," Elani replied, and he did. He had learned from Tūtūpapa what alcohol could do, but he drank anyway.

He had his reasons, or at least that's what he told himself at the time.

"We all do," she said, giving him an out. "Now, come on, let's get you a chair and a bottle of water."

Elani preferred not to embarrass himself further. "Nah, I should just go home already, you know?" He pulled out his cell phone and called Jeff. "I bet that fucker just left me here," Elani walked past her and back inside. He found Jeff propped up in a corner, drool spilling out onto his T-shirt. "Jeff," Elani shook him. "Wake up," he shook him again, this time letting his head bounce against the wall.

"You want me to call someone?" the woman asked him.

"Nah, fuck him," Elani let Jeff slide to the carpet. "He's breathing."

"You up in the dorms?"

Elani nodded, "Bean Hall."

"I can take you," she told him. "I just need to call my sister and we can go."

Elani's forehead screamed. His grandfather's face flashed in front of him: empty, breathless. He thought about Kāʻeo. "No," he let out suddenly. "I'll be fine."

She looked at him and then at Jeff. "He's worse than you, there's no way he's taking you home."

"I said I'm fine," he told her sharply. "Don't worry about it," and then he walked out of the room, not bothering to explain.

By Elani's calculations, campus was a thirty-minute walk away, twenty-five if he maintained a decent pace. He kept to the main road, not wanting to get lost down one of the side streets. Almost there, he kept telling himself, but by the time he hit Agate Street he could feel his perseverance wavering. It didn't help that he had to rest every other block to keep from vomiting on his shoes. He stopped at a bus stop and lay down, hoping to ease his nausea. He didn't dare close his eyes, afraid of what his mind might conjure.

The vision was still with him though, and he wondered if it had been a dream or perhaps something worse. Mark had once told Elani about a recurring nightmare that had haunted him. "Night terrors," Mark had called them, a term that he had borrowed from Lana's notes. Elani's dreams were normally fantastical in nature, in part due, Elani suspected, to his choice of reading material, and if he ever had nightmares, they were far from realistic, but this was different. The vision had been tangible and real. So much so, that when he ran his tongue over his lips he could taste the salt, or when he inhaled, he could feel a strain in his chest, latent but clearly there. He replayed Mark's message over again in his head, and felt the panic in his throat return, thinking about Tūtūpapa motionless and hollow.

A car pulled up to the curb and honked. "The buses stop running at 11." Elani recognized the woman's voice.

Elani thought about dismissing her again, but at his current pace it would probably be morning by the time he got back to his dorm. That, and he could use a diversion, however temporary. He got up and she popped open the car door. "Where's your sister?" he asked, noticing that she was alone.

"She's eating with her friends downtown, didn't even bother to tell me that she left." She looked over at Elani, "My name's Josie, by the way."

"Tony," he said out of habit. "How the hell did you find me?" he asked her.

"I didn't," Josie said. "I was waiting to turn and saw you lying down at the bus stop. You don't see that very often in this neighborhood." At the 19th Avenue intersection, she looked over at him. "So what was up with you back there?" Josie asked. "I mean when you left, you seemed pretty upset. You're not one of those angry drunks, are you?"

"Nah, I don't really drink, I just have an idiot for a roommate, you know?" he said, letting his inflection slip for the second time that night.

She caught it that time. "You from Eugene?" she asked.

"Nope, Hawaii," he said it as flat as possible.

"Must be nice."

"You'd be surprised."

She took the hint. "You have family here, friends?"

"Nah, it's just me." He remained intentionally vague.

"That can be hard," she said, approaching East 15th. She put her signal on. "I remember when I first moved here, it was disorienting not knowing anyone or where anything was."

Elani knew that feeling, especially tonight. "But I thought your sister's here?"

"This is her first year," Josie clarified. "I'm two years older."

"And at a freshman party," he joked.

"See, that's where you're wrong," she raised a finger to explain. "My sister was at the party, I was just looking out for her. Somebody has to."

"But you're only dumb once, right?" Elani remarked sarcastically, borrowing Jeff's line; however hyperbolic, it did the job.

"You would know," she smirked.

Josie pulled to the side and parked. Elani could make out his dorm room window from where they were. He knew what was waiting for him there in the dark, brooding. "So, you're just a stranger, huh?" she asked, leaning on the steering wheel. "Making your way."

"I'm just here for the usual, seeing what's out there, figuring shit out."

"That makes two of us," Josie said, pushing the conversation forward, clearly waiting for Elani to make a move.

Elani wasn't sure what to do next, so he reached for the door. "Thanks for the ride," he told her when he got out. He turned around, realizing his mistake. "Maybe I'll see you around," he said, a question more than a statement, but if he was expecting an answer, she didn't give him one.

"You'll have to find me next time then," Josie told him, offering him another chance. He got up the courage and took it, asking for her number like he had always seen it done on TV. "What's yours?" Josie asked him, and then proceeded to tap it into her phone.

When Elani got back to his room, he had a single text message from Josie, a question mark. A mystery that Elani wasn't sure how to respond to and one that he didn't want to ask about, not yet anyway. Instead, he let his interest trace over the glyph, from the curl of the lobe to the ball and then back again. It was enough to keep him occupied until he slipped into sleep, and to stay that way, until morning when his chest grew tight again.

As the weekend came to a close and the week progressed, Elani thought less and less about the vision. Mark phoned on Sunday to let Elani know that the shelter had been a dead end, but beyond that

Mark stopped calling. On several occasions that week, Elani thought about checking in with his brother, but he didn't see the point. They were both busy with their own lives and they both had better uses for their time than to tread around the topic of their brother's addiction again. He thought about calling Ma, but he didn't want to add to her anxiety. Although Elani remained concerned about his blackout, a quick Internet search yielded the answer that he was looking for, with excessive alcohol consumption being the most likely cause of the previous night's event.

With less time devoted to obsessing over the occurrence, he had more to devote to midterms and his brewing intoxication with Josie, the latter being of far greater interest to him. Having never dated in high school, he was initially unsure about what to make of the situation, but between classes and homework, her text messages and phone calls were a welcome change. Their conversations were light and playful, and they often talked about classes and school, and where Elani had been and where Josie insisted she take him. They joked over iced frappucinos and lunch dates, and studied and hung out whenever they had free time. She was open and honest, an aspect of her personality that Elani admired. She had no shame in talking about the classes that she had withdrawn from or divulging details about the parties where she too had blacked out. She was also confident in her aspirations, in her desire to document the everyday with her camera's lens. Elani on the other hand remained reserved, opening up only when it came to discussions of his goals and his writing, and although she never pressured him to reveal more than he wanted to about his life before Oregon, it didn't stop her from asking.

"You never talk much about your family," Josie had remarked to him one night after dinner. They were sitting on the couch in her apartment, looking through a collection of photographs that she had taken, a project on her grandmother and the blankets that she had woven for Josie and her sister before they were born: the techniques and people and blankets themselves. "Why is that?" she asked. "Do you guys not get along?"

Elani wasn't sure if it was the photographs that prompted the question or the phone calls that he had ignored at dinner. When

Josie had asked about the interruption, he had given her a plausible excuse: probably just his brother nagging him about coming home for Thanksgiving break. He imagined that it was partially true, while the rest he preferred to worry about later. "We all have our issues, what family doesn't?" Elani said, doing his best to remain casual, picking up one of the photographs and holding it up to the light. "Who is this?" Elani asked.

"One of my grandmother's friends, they weave together," Josie explained, before handing him another. "It helps to talk about it."

"There's nothing to talk about," Elani said, concentrating on the photograph, unable to keep it still. He dropped it on the table and hid his hands in the front pocket of his hoodie.

"You sound like my dad," she said, running her hand down the sleeve. "After my mom died, he just shut down, didn't even bother to give us the usual shit about heaven and better places. Never even talked about it with us for years, like it just happened and that was it."

"It's nothing like that," Elani rationalized. "I just like to keep my thoughts on the present," he slipped his hand out of his jacket and laced his fingers with hers. "And whatever's next."

"That doesn't mean it's not there," she told him, nuzzling her head near his neck. "It's like with my dad," she began, clearly not letting the subject go this time. Elani could feel his pulse in his temples. "One day he just came in my room and started crying, he couldn't even tell me why, but he didn't have to." Elani fought back the urge to get up, and instead focused on the noise of Josie's voice. She continued to talk but he couldn't hear her, no matter how hard he listened.

Elani had never seen his father cry, but he heard him once. Elani was nearly asleep when the door to his parents' room opened. At first, he thought it was Ma, but Pops had already made sure that she had taken her medication and would sleep through the night, and then the gasps came, dry and shuddered, and Elani knew that it wasn't Ma in the hallway. He rolled over to face the wall, and the bed creaked just as his father composed himself, and then Pops made his way down the hall and out the door, and Elani heard his father reverse out of the garage, his brakes squealing before he shifted into gear and started down the road.

When Elani saw the lights, he knew that he was back on the plane. He held his breath and unbuckled his seat belt, leaving his grandfather behind. He swam toward an emergency exit on the opposite side, but it wouldn't open. Every one he tried was jammed. He made his way up the rows until he got to the cockpit, but when he shot through the door, he found his father in the pilot's chair, his head buried in the dash. Above the console, there was a hole in the windshield. He went for it, but then a hand grabbed his ankle and pulled him back.

Elani woke up on Josie's couch. He was out of breath, his neck and chest damp with sweat. He wasn't sure when he had passed out, but he was thankful to find that Josie was asleep beside him. He edged his body off the couch and slipped into the bathroom, not bothering to turn the light on. He washed his face in the basin and glanced at the shadow in the mirror, the reflection a murky mass of blacks and grays. "Tony?" Josie called out drowsily.

"I'm not feeling so great," he told her when he came out.

"I figured," she said. "You just kind of knocked out."

"It's been a long week," he told her. "That test for Wallace's class really killed me."

"You want me to make you some tea?"

"Nah, I think I'm just going to go home," he replied.

"Let me grab my keys."

"I'll be fine," he went for the door.

"Anthony," she was peeking over the couch cushions at him, a grin deepening the dimples in her cheeks. "I don't want to spend the rest of my night driving by bus stops, hunting you down," she said. He acted like he didn't hear her and returned her smile, accepting her offer for the sake of the ruse. But on the ride to his dorm room, Elani remained silent, pretending that it was nausea and not the vision that was making it difficult for him to breathe.

"Da police stay looking fo Kāʻeo," Mark said. They had come by the house, asking questions: *When was the last time Mark had seen him? Did he have any other family he could be staying with? Friends?* The police never said why, but they gave Mark their information and let him know to call them if he ever showed up. Mark had his suspicions; Junior's father had been arrested a few days before. "Elani? You dea or what?" Mark's voice broke through the silence. "Elani?" He turned off his phone.

Elani didn't sleep that night or the next. When Josie came around to check on him, to ask why she couldn't get in touch with him, to ask why he wasn't returning her calls, Elani told her that he was feeling worse. It was the truth, and thankfully his lack of sleep supported his condition. But without Josie, all he had left to divert his attention away from his anxiety was Jeff and school, and he saw no shelter in the former, at least not one that didn't involve intoxication of some degree. So in the hopes of staying afloat, Elani committed himself to marathon study sessions on the fourth floor of the Knight Library before class, and afterwards, rather than coming back to his dorm, he roamed the busiest parts of campus or wandered around downtown, until he came home to either get a jump on upcoming deadlines or to listen to Jeff's stoned ramblings on the aesthetics of the Cheeto, crunchy not puffed.

He did his best to stave off the visions, sleeping in short shifts to avoid them, but they eventually became more and more frequent, and began to spill out into the real world. On several occasions, Elani had woken up on the floor, his bed disheveled, and Jeff would tell Elani about how he had come home to find him thrashing at the air or clawing at the walls. During lectures, Elani felt restless and uneasy, and every few minutes he would find himself taking inventory of the exits, his eyes darting back and forth between the windows and the doors. Even his writing began to suffer, the work that he was producing uninspired and incomprehensible. He began to wonder what the point was anymore.

Although at times his efforts yielded results, Elani able to get through his work with little trouble or enjoy a nap in the afternoon, he knew it was only a matter of time before Mark called to let him know that their brother was dead, to affirm the disquiet that was swallowing Elani night and day. And then a week before break, while Elani was looking over an essay for one of his classes, he answered his phone. He was surprised that Mark would call him so late, but at the same time it wouldn't have been the first instance that his brother had forgotten the time difference. "I know you don't want to hear this, but I really am busy," Elani said, circling a paragraph that he needed to refine. "Unless this is important, can I call you back?"

Mark didn't answer immediately. Instead Elani heard what he thought was sniffling on the other end, his brother clearing his throat. "Elani," Mark finally got out. "I stay sorry fo calling you so late but…" Elani dropped his cellphone, recognizing the tone in his brother's voice. It was the same one that Pops had used when he had called Mark to tell him about Tūtūpapa, and the same one that the doctor had used when she came out of the emergency room to update the family on Pops' status. Elani left his keys and his phone on the bed, and walked out the door.

Elani had no destination in mind. He walked across campus, passing the University Health Center, the brick building closed for the evening, dark at that hour. The streetlights led him up Riverfront Parkway, and he stopped at the bridge that overlooked the Eugene Millrace. The manmade channel was tepid and slow, like the drip of an IV. Elani remembered how resolute Tūtūpapa had been about his treatment and about the possibility of living on—in the beginning, always retelling survivor stories that he had heard from veterans that he had sat with and who had seen others come and go—and how quickly it took for Tūtūpapa's resolve to subside. He remembered standing in the corner of Tūtūpapa's hospital room, eyes closed, while the rest of his family cried and prayed. Elani remembered Tūtūpapa's funeral, walking up to the casket but refusing to look into the box.

He continued on the road, down Riverfront and between the guardrails leading him to the Bascom Bike Path. Elani thought of Pops then, and about the night of his father's car crash. Elani had been in his bedroom, reading, when he had heard the heavy thud of his father's footsteps on the tile floor. Elani had wanted to tell his father not to leave, that there was nothing out there for Pops to find, but he didn't. Instead, Elani did what he always had done: he put his head down and read until his eyes went blurry from fatigue, trusting that eventually his father would stop, and then just after he fell asleep, the hospital called. Elani walked along the Willamette River, thinking about how he couldn't even stay by his father's side the day that they pulled the plug, how he had just walked out and stared into the trash bin until it was over because he just didn't want to admit that his father was gone.

By the time he reached the Ferry Street Bridge, it was almost dawn. Elani was exhausted, empty. His eyes were red, his cheeks were sore, and his throat was dry. He stood at the railing and looked down into the violent rush below him. He placed his hands on the rail to steady his body and took inventory of his regrets. He relived the day that Kāʻeo had moved out, and rehearsed what he could have said to him to convince him to stay. He recalled the night before Tūtūpapa's funeral, and thought about everything that he could have done to wake his brother up. He thought about his time in Oregon and imagined the opportunities that he might have had, the chance encounters that might have occurred if he had stayed home, the possibilities for him to make a difference in his brother's life, however minute. "I'm sorry," he got out, his voice hoarse and unstable. "I'm sorry," he said again, louder this time, his apology echoing in the dead air. He stepped forward and felt his body grow light.

Elani was on the plane again, but he was in no rush to escape. He kissed his grandfather's forehead and then headed for the cockpit. There wasn't much that he could do for Pops, but free his head from the panel and close his eyelids. Elani swam up through the windshield, taking his time, and when he felt the fingers close around his ankle, he didn't fight back, rather he turned to face Kāʻeo, but it wasn't his brother that he saw when he looked down. *Elani*, Kāʻeo's voice surrounded him. *Elani*, it was closer this time. *Elani*, right behind him, he turned around, and Kāʻeo came to him and leaned in, whispering in Elani's ear.

"Wake up."

He opened his eyes to find that he was still on the bridge. It was morning and it had begun to rain, thin pinpoints of light dropping down and blessing his face. Josie was standing over him. "Are you okay?" she asked him.

Elani couldn't explain it, but he felt lighter. "Yeah," Elani told her and then got to his feet. "What're you doing here?" he asked.

"I was worried. I came by your room and Jeff told me that you left your phone and your keys. I called to check in again and he said you still hadn't come home, so I thought I'd drive around and look for you.

I figured you couldn't get very far."

"You were wrong," he let out a small smile.

She smoothed back his hair. "I thought you were going to fall right over the rail," she said. "What happened?"

"Can we talk about it later?" he asked her before realizing that he had already made her wait long enough. "Tonight," he said. "Promise."

She nodded. "Let's get you home," she said, leading him over to her car.

When he got back to his room, Elani was glad to see that he had the dorm to himself. He showered and changed and then he called Mark back, knowing now that he should have done it sooner. His brother didn't answer, but he didn't expect him to. It was still early there. "Call me back when you get this," Elani told him, but then he took it back. "You know what, never mind, I'll call you again in a few hours," he said, and turned the volume up on the ringer.

Before Elani got into bed, he sat down and tried to transcribe the words that Kāʻeo had whispered to him. When Elani had heard them, it was as if he had immediately understood what his brother was telling him, but now, all he could remember was reverberations. He transposed several possibilities before he realized that he would need more than time to understand what Kāʻeo had said.

His phone rang. It was Mark. He dropped his pen and picked up. "Hey, I'm sorry about earlier," Elani began to ramble. "I jus—"

Mark didn't answer immediately, and when he did his voice was measured and hesitant. "Da police," Mark began, "dey wen find Kāʻeo."

While Mark told Elani what he knew from the police, Elani pulled up the news on his computer to find out more about what had happened to their brother. An eyewitness said that at about eight p.m. two nights before, a man matching Kāʻeo's description was leaving the 7-Eleven near Wailea Street, when another man got out of a nearby truck and followed him. They argued, Kāʻeo pushing the other man away before continuing to walk quickly down Kalanianaʻole Highway. At that point, the witness said, the other man got back in the passenger side of the truck and started to follow Kāʻeo down the road. When Kāʻeo ducked into Waimānalo Beach Park, the truck parked on the opposite side of the street, pulling as far off as possible. Two men stepped out to the highway and crossed the road.

Kāʻeo's body told the rest. The autopsy report noted bruising and lacerations on his face and torso, suggesting blunt trauma, and the wounds on his hands indicated that he had fought back. Another witness in the area reported hearing three gunshots, but there was only a single entrance wound to the back of Kāʻeo's skull, through the occipital bone. And although they had found gunpowder residue on Kāʻeo's hands, the police did not recover a firearm at the scene.

Elani got up and started to pace. "Do they know who did it?"

"Who you think?" There was only one answer, at least for them. "Junior's faddah stay locked up, Junior stay out on bail. I surprised dat fuckah never try fo start shit wit me."

"This is fucking bullshit," Elani spit out. "What the fuck did Kāʻeo ever do?" They both knew.

"Shit no matter, Elani, dey going get Junior, keh? And if not, I going fucking get him, I promise you dat," Mark assured him. "You jus need fo take care of what you need fo take care of. No need rush, come wen can. I get dis shit under control."

Elani didn't want to think about the outcome of his brother's aggression. "Don't do anything stupid," he advised him.

"You sound like Ma," Mark replied.

Elani swallowed his own anger, "We've lost enough." Mark agreed. "What the fuck was he doing in Waimānalo anyway?" Elani asked, continuing to work through the details.

"I dunno," Mark replied. "Da lady down 7-Eleven said he was always in and out of dea, dat he wen work at one farm up da road."

"A farm?" Elani asked skeptically. "Are they sure it's Kāʻeo?"

"He wen have his wallet on him," Mark confirmed a detail that the news hadn't mentioned. "And I wen see him already, Elani," Mark reminded him, his voice sinking. "Stay Kāʻeo."

"Have you gone down to the farm yet?"

"I going check um out Monday," Mark said.

"Wait for me," Elani told him, needing to see it for himself. "I want to go with you."

"What about sku?"

He looked at his calendar, "I'm going to email my professors, plus break's coming up, I'm not going to miss anything." Not that it mattered anyway.

"You need money?" Mark asked.

"I still have some left over from my student loans," Elani did the math.

"You need anything, jus let me know den, keh?"

"I'll call you when I have my ticket," Elani said, picking up his laptop again and beginning his search for flights.

There was a quiet then, Elani's fingers snapping at the keyboard, while his brother remained on the other end, listening intently. "Elani, stay okay fo be upset," Mark told him, knowing his brother well.

Elani took his fingers off of the keys and waited for the prices to load. "I know," he finally replied, staring at the screen until he couldn't.

Over the next day, Elani prepared for his flight home. The earliest departure that he could find was the Sunday red-eye. He had just enough to pay for a one-way fare, figuring that he could get his brother to purchase the return flight when he was ready to leave. As expected, his professors responded to his correspondence with genuine concern, providing him with assignment instructions and deadline extensions, and he assured all of them that he would turn in his work as soon as he got back, though he intentionally left out a return date or lack thereof.

That night, Elani went over to Josie's apartment to explain to her not only why he was leaving, but also about his family and about the morning that she had found him at the bridge. Elani told her everything, a little at a time. With each detail, Elani could feel the character that he had made of himself being edited out. Josie listened intently, never pulling back when Elani expected her to, and when he was finished, she held him until his heart slowed.

"Are you going to come back?" Josie asked him before he left.

"I don't know," he answered her honestly. "I can't really think about that right now."

"Either way," she said, "you call me, okay?" Elani promised her that he would, knowing that he owed her at least that much.

On the plane ride home, Elani was restless, but it wasn't grief keeping him awake this time; it was the vision of his brother. Kāʻeo's words still eluded Elani. And even though it was constantly on his mind, the vision never returned. He took the napkin from under his plastic cup and wrote a string of words. An incomprehensible attempt at his brother's fluid Hawaiian, but an attempt nonetheless. He would figure it out. He had to.

When Elani got to Honolulu, Mark was waiting to take him to Kahaluʻu. The first stretch of the ride was several miles of false starts and awkward pauses. Although they had spoken more over the past two days than they had over the last three months, there was still a distance between them. By the time they got on the H-3, Elani had figured it was best to just pretend that he was sleeping. At least then he wouldn't have to field another question about the flight or school. "We some sad Pordagees, you know dat?" Mark said before Elani could close his eyes. "Sitting hea like two haoles at one bus stop."

"You sound surprised," Elani quipped, resting his head against the seat back.

"Nah, I jus wen figgah you was done wit all dis, you know? Da whole vow of silence," Mark replied. "But I guess you was always quiet, ah?"

Elani ignored the comment. "It's been a long night," he said, crossing his arms.

"Been plenny long nights, ah?" Mark added. "Das how things been fo one while now."

"What's your point?"

"I jus like know how you doing, das all."

"Like I said, school's on hold but I'm not worried about it." He turned his head to face the window, "I'm just tired."

"Fuck all dat, Elani," Mark replied. "I talking hea, you know?" He touched his chest.

Elani waited until after they were out of the tunnel to respond. "Still processing," Elani told Mark. "But I'm better than I was."

"First Papa, den Pops, and now—"

"Like you said, we've been through a lot of long nights," Elani interrupted, seeing no reason for him to continue.

"Well, I glad you hea," Mark replied. Elani taking it for what it was, his brother's last attempt. "Glad everybody together fo a change."

He turned from the window. "How's Ma doing with everything?" Elani asked, knowing that the news must be wearing on her more than any of them.

"Hard fo say right now," Mark shifted in his seat. "But she stay strong, she stay holding on. Helps dat we stay home wit her, ah? And dat she still going therapy. She get one appointment tomorrow. Lana going take her."

"I figured she would just be..." Elani trailed off, remembering what it was like after Tūtūpapa had died. "I guess I didn't know what to expect."

Mark nodded, "I think after everything dat wen happen dis last year she jus wen realize da kine, dat she no can lose herself li'dat again. Plus, I think she like da company, ah? Me and Lana and Aunty Sheryl. Always get one of us wit her."

"She's getting better then?"

"I think so," Mark responded confidently. "She get her days, but not like befo. She even talking about going back work, you know? Come January she going try."

"And what about you guys? What about Lana, she doesn't mind?"

"Nothing more important than family, she knows dat, and as long as I stay good, she no care. Plus, I think she like all da time she spend wit Ma. Now she get somebody else fo analyze besides me."

Elani let out a grin. "And what about you?" he asked, not sure if his brother was avoiding the topic or not.

"I get one new job, you know? Working construction fo one of Pops' friends. Lana get me looking into night sku classes. You can picture—"

"With all of this, I mean," Elani interjected.

Mark kept his attention on the road. "I stay doing okay right now. Was pretty bad dat first night though. Still pretty bad wen I think about everything," Mark admitted. "After I wen talk to da cops, I wen drive over to Junior's place and jus wen camp dea couple hours, you know? I jus wanted fo kill dat fuckah so bad. I mean, I still like one chance fo murder dat fuckah, but like I wen tell you already, he going get what stay coming to him. I wen tell da fucking cops everything, you know? No way dat bastard going get away wit da shit dat he wen do to Kāʻeo."

Elani found comfort in that. "Honestly, I would do anything to talk to him again," Elani voiced his grief. "Ask him about everything, you know? Not just about that night, but about before, about him and Papa, about him and Pops. I guess I just want to understand."

"Da kine he was going through," Mark eased onto the exit to Kāneʻohe town. "I dunno if we ever going understand dat."

"What do you think it was?" Elani asked, wanting to know his brother's theory, but if Mark had one, he didn't share it with Elani.

"Not going change what wen happen to him," Mark remained stoic. "Only can accept dat nutten going bring him back and try fo move on." Elani disagreed.

"How did it go when you talked with him?" Elani asked. It was another question that he had been thinking about on the plane, knowing that Mark had a chance that none of them had. "That last time."

"What you mean?"

"I mean, what did you say to him?"

"I wen tell him da truth," Mark answered candidly, doing his best to be forthcoming with Elani. "I told him dat I wen let my own shit get in da way, you know? I wen tell him dat I was sorry fo dat."

"You think it made a difference?" Elani asked, turning to his brother.

"Stay three C's fo wen you get one loved one on drugs," Mark began, knowing well the ghost that was haunting Elani. "You never cause da addiction, you no can cure da addiction, and you no can control da addiction, but you know what? No matter how many times I wen hear dat, no matter how many times I wen say da words…"

"You did everything you could," Elani reassured him.

"You think so?" Mark asked, throwing a glance at his brother. Elani nodded. It was one of the few things that he was certain of.

By the time Elani and Mark got to the house, Lana and Ma were asleep, but the lights were on and a plate of leftovers was in the microwave waiting for them. Elani wasn't hungry. "So I guess I've got the couch then?" Elani asked Mark, walking from the kitchen and into the living room, where the furniture had been replaced and rearranged, blankets and quilts folded on the ottoman. Rather than dust and moist leather, he could smell lemon and dryer sheets, and a hint of pīkake coming in from the front yard.

"We wen make a few changes, ah?" Mark walked past him and opened the curtain in front of the sliding glass door. The lānai had been reduced; the house extended so there was room for another bedroom. "Me and couple friends been working on um. Not pau yet, but stay good enough fo me and Lana right now."

"A few changes, huh?" Elani raised an eyebrow.

"No worry," Mark said. "We never touch your room."

To Elani's surprise, his brother wasn't exaggerating. It was as if he had never left: drafts strewn across his desk, old notes pinned to the corkboard on the wall, a paperback turned over on his bedside table, yellowed and open. He walked inside and nearly tripped over a towel on the floor, one of the many that he had used to block the space at the bottom of the door. "I don't remember it being such a mess in here,"

Elani remarked, dropping his backpack on the rug.

"Ma wen come in hea couple times, but das all," Mark commented. "Oddah than dat, stay da same hole you wen burrow yourself in."

"I can see that," Elani replied, making a mental note to sort through it all.

Mark propped one arm up and peeked his head inside. "I wen give da farm one call today," he said abruptly. "Going head out dea early. You still like go or what?"

"Yeah," Elani replied, glad to have the chance.

Mark nodded. "You like me shut da door?" he asked.

"Leave it open," Elani told him and then wished his brother good night.

After he showered and changed, Elani laid in the dark and listened to the geckos that clung to his window screen. He watched the curtains billow like apparitions, the breeze coming into the room and out into the hallway, knocking the door to Kāʻeo's bedroom gently against the jamb. Elani saw no point in ignoring it now and no reason why he should. He didn't find much inside: a drawer full of Kāʻeo's old school work and other junk that his brother had collected over time, a closet of discarded clothes that Kāʻeo had left behind, wire hangers, and an empty shelf. He leafed through the books on his brother's desk, finding only silverfish and a loose bookmark. Not even a dog-ear or a stray annotation, no signs of life. He didn't know what he was looking for, but whatever it was, it wasn't there.

By the time Elani finally drifted off, a shrill crowing told him that it was morning. Mark was already up and at the table, Ma was scrambling eggs and frying SPAM. She wiped her hands on the dishrag and gave Elani a kiss on each cheek. Her hair was a straw nest and Elani could see a ribbon of Kleenex hanging out of her robe. "You like rice?" she asked him, running her hands down his shoulders. He shook his head and hugged her. "You boys be safe today, ah?" Ma advised them, scooping a helping of eggs onto Elani's plate. "And I like you call wen you get dea."

"We going be fine, Ma," Mark assured her, paying her concern no mind.

"You find anything else out?" Elani asked after he took a seat at the table.

"Da guy never say much," Mark dug up a forkful of ketchup and rice. "He was sorry fo hear about Kāʻeo. Dat he was going get his things together fo us."

"Things?" Elani looked up from his plate.

"I never ask," Mark replied, fueling Elani's curiosity. "I jus like get out dea and see fo ourselves, you know? I still no even understand what he was doing out dea anyway."

"Whatever your braddah was doing, he wen have one reason," Ma added. "Das how Kāʻeo was."

"Even in college," Elani nodded, remembering the dirt that always trailed from the door to Kāʻeo's room and the lectures that his brother would often give, though Elani's mind had always been lost in his imagination.

"Your braddah was one stubborn boy, but he was always determined, you know? He always wen try fo do da right thing." She reached for the tissue in her pocket but remained stoic, leaving it there.

Is that what this was about? Elani wondered. Only Kāʻeo would know.

After they ate, Elani and Mark headed for Waimānalo. Elani didn't remember the last time that he had been to that part of Oʻahu, but Mark made sure to remind him. "Was one of Pops' union parties, one family potluck," he waxed nostalgic.

It came back to him. "With the mayonnaise salad," Elani joined in.

"Eh, was couple pieces potato in dea."

"I don't think I puked more in my life."

Mark bounced in his seat, "And you was too shame fo go shower da shit off and too da kine fo jump in da water."

"There was jellyfish," Elani defended his younger self.

"Was always something wit you, Elani: jellyfish, or coral, or rocks."

"There were, you know that."

But Mark's mind had left that shore for another. "Kāʻeo was li'dat too, you know, wen he was little. Scared of losing one toe or getting coral in his foot, das what Papa wen tell me anyway, wen I was learning fo swim."

"Fucking amazing, the way Kāʻeo swam."

"Fuckah was one beast in da water," Mark admitted. "Wen he was out dea, he never like leave."

"Why do you think he loved it so much?" Elani asked, following his brother's direction. "Fuck, why did you go out there every time? You didn't even stand a chance."

"Eh, was couple times," Mark slapped Elani's shoulder.

"That you got close maybe," Elani testified.

"Das da kine right dea, ah?" Mark submitted. "I never like let him win. I never like give him da satisfaction."

"I don't think he cared about that," Elani said.

"Nah," Mark shook his head. "But he never wen ack li'dat, you know?" Elani had to give him that.

They drove through Waimānalo until they reached the dirt road that they were looking for. At the end of the driveway, a tall man in dusted jeans and a wash-worn T-shirt was waiting for them. "Jarrett," he introduced himself, greeting them both with a close handshake, calloused and firm. Elani couldn't help but be reminded of their father. "Like I told you on the phone, I really was sorry to hear about your brother," he said, leading them up the driveway and deeper into the farm. "He was a good kid, a hard worker."

"How long was he working here?" Elani asked, shading his face with his right hand.

Jarrett pulled at his beard. "July, August maybe," he replied. "But we had met before, I knew one of his professors, Dr. Laurie Kauhane, you know her?" Elani didn't recognize the name but he recorded it in his head. "He had a real passion for the work he was doing out here," Jarrett added, passing a field of dry land kalo. "Had a real sense for it, too."

"You know wea he was staying?" Mark inquired before Elani could.

Jarrett pointed down the path, at a wooden shed the size of their parents' garage "I told him I had a room, but he said he liked it out here. He had electricity, a roof over his head, plenty of space. Plus, I think he liked to wander around at night, he even slept up the mountain sometimes. I caught him a couple mornings coming down from there."

"What was he doing?"

"No idea," Jarrett replied, "but he found plenty of ways to occupy his time." He walked over to the double doors and unhooked the latch. When Jarrett opened them up, Elani wasn't sure what to say. "The inside still needs some work, but it's a hell of a lot better than when we picked it up."

"What the fuck did he want with a boat?" Elani exclaimed. Mark walked past him and slid his hand over the fiberglass. In the light, Elani could see that the hull was smooth and freshly sanded, but other than that, he didn't see the significance.

"Can get my truck back hea?" Mark asked Jarrett, jumping up on the trailer to look inside.

"I'll tow it out for you," Jarrett said. "No problem."

Elani waited for an answer from one of them. "Do you know what he was doing with this?" he asked Mark.

Mark just stared. "Stay one long story," he finally responded. "Can tell you on da ride home."

Elani walked past Mark and looked around the shed. It was bare: a cot in one corner and a variety of farm tools propped up and hanging. Elani stepped back outside. "Was there anything else?" he was desperate.

Jarrett nodded. "I got a box of his things up at the house, clothes mostly. I'll bring it out to your truck."

"That's it?" Elani sputtered. "Just this dinghy and some clothes?"

"Come on," Mark interrupted Elani before he could embarrass himself. "We need fo get dis home."

When they got back to the truck, Mark pled guilty to finding Kāʻeo out in the driveway the night before Tūtūpapa's funeral, and told him about the keys that had been left out on his dash. "I jus wen throw dem in my glove box," he said, expanding on what he had already told Elani about his conversation with Kāʻeo. "And den after dat night in da hospital, after Kāʻeo wen leave rehab, I wen check again, ah? And dey was gone." Mark confessed that although he had hoped that Kāʻeo had held on to them, he was surprised to see that he had.

Elani understood. It didn't matter what the police told them now. "He was clean," Elani said, overwhelmed by Mark's story.

"He was clean," Mark affirmed Elani's conclusion, wiping his face.

Back at their house, Elani took the box that Jarrett had given them into his bedroom, while Mark dealt with the boat in the garage. Elani undid the flaps and inventoried what was left of their brother. As Jarrett said, it was mostly clothes: two T-shirts, a long-sleeved shirt, board shorts, and a pair of jeans. He found the keys that Mark had told him about, two of them on a single ring, attached to a thick piece of cord, tied tightly at the ends to make a necklace. A guide to boat repair, stamped *Property of the Waimānalo Public Library, removed from circulation* and a *.25* written on the title page. And then under the guide, he found a single-subject spiral notebook, 100 pages, college-ruled, and then below it another. He opened the first one and saw his brother's handwriting, sharp and bold.

I not alone, Kāʻeo wrote to no one but himself. *I get one purpose, I get one family, I not alone.* Although there was much for Elani to discern from Kāʻeo's journals, it was clear to him that what his brother was writing about was more than just his reflections on addiction and sobriety. Interspersed through Kāʻeo's stream of conciousness were references to cultural and political theory, with Tūtūpapa and meth mentioned in the same paragraphs as critics that Elani had heard his brother talk about but that he had never been interested in. He took note of words that he couldn't define, both Hawaiian and English alike, and started to fill in the margins with annotations, question marks or his own thoughts on his brother's perspectives. When he encountered sections of text that he couldn't make out, he would list possibilities above or below or in-between. Entries often took up several pages, with no clear insight into what might have drawn Kāʻeo to write them, but in every case, they ended in the same way: *I get one family, I get one purpose, I not alone.*

It was morning by the time he finally found what he was looking for. He didn't recognize the words at first. In fact, he passed over them, distracted by the mention of Tūtūpapa's brother, a granduncle that Elani had never known about, and the familiarity of the mantra that accompanied them. He wasn't sure if it was fatigue getting the better of him, so he read the page again and discovered the whispers. He sounded them out just to be sure. A test that he practiced every time he came across a sentence in Hawaiian. "O ka makapō—" he stopped and started again. "O ka makapō wale no ka mea hā—" he stuttered. "O ka makapō wale no ka mea hāpapa i ka pōuli." He repeated it back slower, taking time to inhale and exhale. "O ka makapō wale no ka mea hāpapa i ka pōuli."

Elani stood up and walked to where Kāʻeo had been standing the day that he moved out for good. *"O ka makapō wale no ka mea hāpapa i ka pōuli,"* Kāʻeo had said to Elani on that day and in his dream. *"You need fo take da time fo figgah your shit out or you not going nowea,"* Kāʻeo had told him, but he was always so passionate, so confident in what he was doing. *"One day you going ask yourself wea you going and you going know why I stay doing dis. Den you going know our truth fo yourself."* Elani still didn't understand, but he knew that there might be someone that could help.

"Can I borrow your truck?" Elani asked Mark after breakfast. "I want to run an errand."

"Dis get something fo do wit da notebooks?" he asked, handing over his keys to Elani.

"Not exactly," Elani told him. "I'll let you know when I get back."

Before Elani left, he made sure to check that Dr. Laurie Kauhane was still teaching at the university. With morning traffic, he got to her classroom just in time to miss her. "You can try her office, but I know she had an appointment downtown at 10:45," her TA told him.

"That's alright," Elani said. He had already been there. "Maybe I'll try the library instead."

"I don't know if you had a specific question for her, but I might be able to help."

It couldn't hurt.

Elani unzipped his backpack and showed her Kāʻeo's notebook. He flipped through until he found the page. "I'm still going through all of this," Elani began. "But I heard my brother say this once and I'm trying to figure out what it means."

She glanced over the handwriting and took the notebook from him. "Where did you get this?" she asked him, thumbing through the pages.

"My brother," Elani replied, surprised by her interest.

"Give me a second," she said, walking over to her computer before he could respond. "It's been awhile and I just want to be sure." After several clicks and keystrokes, she took out a pen and a Post-it. "It's an ʻōlelo noʻeau, a Hawaiian proverb," she explained, writing it out clearer than Kāʻeo had written it. "Literally, only the blind grope in the darkness," she translated, sticking the note to the page.

"What does that mean exactly?" he asked, missing the implication.

"Essentially, without a sense of purpose, you're not going to get much done; or if you have no direction in life, you'll go nowhere." She looked down at the notebook and passed it back to him. "Nowadays it's easy to get lost, but you need to remember what matters."

Elani sat down at one of the desks and thought about what his brother had told him and about his dream. "And what's that?"

"Depends on the person," she said, deciphering his demeanor. "Are you and your brother close?" she asked him, hoping to make sense of the situation.

"Not really," Elani admitted. "He was six older than me. Not to mention, all of this," Elani tapped the notebook and read his brother's words again. "I never cared much for any of it really. Never understood it or him. Maybe that was the problem, I never gave myself the chance to, you know?" Or maybe we never had a chance to begin with. He ran his fingers along the lines, navigating the imprints that his brother had left with his pen, *O ka makapō wale no ka mea hāpapa i ka pōuli*. So we have to find our own way, he thought, but we can't lose sight of what came before, where we came from. Elani looked up, realizing that he had been lost in his thoughts. "Sorry, I'm still working out all of this."

"Did something happen to him?" she stumbled.

"I'm sorry?" he was confused. His mind was still on the notes in front of him.

"Kā—" She stopped herself. A half-pause. He wasn't sure if he had heard her right. "Your brother, I mean, did something happen to him?" she let out. "I'm sorry," she waved off the question. "It's none of my business. Leave your email and I'll let Dr. Kauhane know that you came by."

"Did you know him?" he asked, thinking about whether or not his brother had ever mentioned a woman other than their mother in his writing. "You might have had him in one of your classes," he continued, eager for another perspective. "Kāʻeo Teixeira."

"We were friends."

It was Elani's turn to collect his words. "He passed away last week," he said, but that wasn't right. "I mean, there was an accident," he gave it another try, not realizing how hard it would be to say it aloud.

"An accident?" she asked him.

That couldn't have been further from the truth. "Not at all," he finally told her, clasping his hands together in front of his face and letting his forehead rest against his fingers.

She didn't push him any further. "He was interested in the language," she broke the silence between them, "and moʻolelo, but he especially loved caring for the land. He used to talk about how connected it made him feel." She rested her hands on the desk behind her and stared at the chalkboard, drawing memories from the dust. "We worked one summer up in the mountains," she continued. "Our truths are in the stories and in the land, he had told me once. Parts of ourselves that we can hold on our tongues and in our hands." Elani wrote down what she said, just below his brother's last entry, and for the first time he noticed how similar their handwriting was.

"I'm realizing that there's a lot I didn't know about him," he confessed, knowing that there were still so many questions that he had about Kāʻeo's life. He knew that it would take him at least a few more days to get through the rest of his brother's writing and far longer to digest it all. "More that I wish I did."

"I actually have some books you might want to take a look at," she said, leading him out the door. "I can email you a list of other resources, send you what I remember from back then."

"If you think it will help," he replied, following her down the hallway. He hoped it would. They walked out of the classroom and up to her office. "What was your name again?" Elani asked her when they got to her floor, not sure if she had introduced herself or not. "I'm Elani."

"Chloe," she replied, and then unlocked her door and let him in.

Rather than observe Thanksgiving, the Teixeiras took the day to plan Kāʻeo's celebration of life. Over bowls of Ma's Portuguese bean soup, Mark and Lana called Father Dumadag to reserve the church hall and spoke with Aunty Sheryl to arrange for her husband to cater the event. It was to be an intimate affair, but they planned for more than just friends and family, extending invitations to anyone who knew Kāʻeo and wanted to join in on the commemoration of his memory. With the logistics taken care of, Elani sought to memorialize his brother in a way that he knew Kāʻeo would have appreciated.

"So going be like one mural or something?" Mark inquired when Elani told them about his idea.

"More like a collage or a mosaic," Elani expanded on his explanation, though he knew none of those words captured the extent of his undertaking. While reading through the books that Chloe had given him, Elani recognized a concept that Kāʻeo had mentioned in his journals—makawalu—and thought about the series of photographs that Josie had made, conceiving of a way to preserve his brother in the same way that she had her grandmother and her heritage. "I want to show everything that he is," Elani explained further. "His life from every perspective." Mark still wasn't clear about what Elani had planned, but he welcomed Elani's venture regardless.

"We can set up an area in the center of the hall," Lana made a note. "Maybe a couple tables for you to organize everything."

"You going need pictures," Ma jumped in. "Come," she said, waving Elani into the hallway. She opened the closet and took down several shoeboxes full of envelopes of glossy images. He dropped them in the center of his room and returned for the rest. "Get more above da washer," she told Elani.

"I want everything," he replied, anxious to get started.

The next morning, he called Josie to ask her advice on how to go about implementing his idea. "Take the time to plan it out," she advised him, encouraged by the inspiration that he had found. "You have the concept, but you need to think about what you want to capture about your brother. What do you want to say about him?"

"I'm still working on that," Elani replied.

"Well give yourself some time," she said. "And keep your camera on you, just in case," she stopped herself. "Wait, do you have a camera?" Elani laughed. "I have one you can use," she told him. "I can mail it to you tomorrow."

"I can't take that," he replied.

"Why not?"

"I just—"

"You can give it back to me when I see you," she threw in before he could finish.

He was too struck to respond. She didn't need more than the possibility, knowing that he would answer when he was ready to. "Take as many photos as you can," she picked up where she had left off, "but don't waste too much time on the same shots. Experiment but never erase, you never know what you might find later. You might even consider using your phone, seeing what that change might bring."

"I'm thinking about doing more than just the photographs," Elani spoke up. "I want to include his voice, his experience."

"His writing?" she asked.

"I think so."

"What about sound? Video?" she asked, following his muse.

"We have a few home movies, but nothing that I think would fit in."

"It doesn't have to be him," she replied. "If you're going to include his voice, what about yours? Mark's? Your mother's?" He grabbed a pen and a piece of paper and started to map out his ideas, suddenly lost in concentration. "It's like you're seeing yourself for the first time, isn't it?" she asked him. "It's like you've become aware of this whole other world that you've always belonged to, this larger part of who you are." She was right. He grabbed another piece of paper and let his thoughts spill over onto the other.

In anticipation of the project, Elani had cleared off his desk and corkboard, posting his approach out across the latter. He had originally imagined three large presentation boards, each one anchored by a part of the mantra that Kāʻeo had used over and over again in his writing. But as he worked through the boxes of photographs that Ma had given him and continued to develop what he wanted to include, he realized that his aspirations were much larger than when he had first conceived them. "I'm going to need at least six tables," Elani told Lana the next morning, "and plenty of space."

Over the next several weeks, Elani used Josie's camera and a voice recorder to document the parts of Kāʻeo's life that few had seen. He drove back out to Waimānalo and toured the farm with Jarrett. He emailed Dr. Kauhane and drove out to her house, using the opportunity to take in the small cottage where his brother had worked and the adjacent grounds, being sure to walk up and down the river that his brother had written about. Chloe even introduced Elani to a few of Kāʻeo's old classmates, including Alakaʻi, an activist studying environmental law. "He was an intense guy," Alakaʻi told Elani. "When he committed himself to something, there was no half-way. He wanted to be better, to do better, and he never stopped pushing himself or those around him because that's how he was."

For the section of the mural that Elani wanted to dedicate to the family, Elani asked Ma to help him identify the individuals that he couldn't. While they worked through the stack, she talked about when she had first met Pops. "Was one double date. Your faddah was wit one real high makamaka girl—"

"Wait, you weren't on the date together?" Elani interrupted, having never heard the story before.

"I was wit John Lau. One pretty face, but nutten going on inside dat head of his. Your faddah though, he never leave da Pordagee at home dat night. But I wen like da kine," she clarified. "Dat confidence in him." She picked up a photograph of their wedding and laughed. "Look at da two of dem," she pointed at the best man and the maid of honor. "Johnny boy and Miss Christine."

Halfway through another box, Ma shared a faded Polaroid of her mother, who had been born on Hawai'i Island and whose family had once cared for several acres of land there before moving to O'ahu. "What happened to all of it?" Elani asked, taking the photo from her.

"Never have nobody fo care fo all dat," Ma told him. "Was mo better fo jus sell um." She reached for it, tapping the mango tree in the background. "Da best mangos she ever wen eat," Ma said. "She never wen eat anada one again."

When they were done going through the albums and envelopes, Ma took Elani into her room and showed her a picture that she had kept by her mirror. It was a photograph of Tūtūpapa and another man—"your Uncle Joseph"—that she had found in Kā'eo's room after he had moved out of the house. "In his heart, I think your Papa always wanted you guys fo know him," Ma passed him the photograph.

"Kā'eo mentioned him once," Elani told her, noticing the boat in the background. "He didn't say much about him. They were different, but they both fought for what they believed in."

"Your Papa never like talk about his braddah much," Ma said, "but he wen tell me one time dat after your uncle wen pass away, he wen realize dat da fights dey wen have together was fo nutten, was jus him fighting against himself, you understand? Cuz family stay family, no matter what, and witout family, what you get?"

"Nothing," Elani said, adding the image to the collection.

After they had gone through every last box, Elani went outside to take pictures of the neighborhood. He went down the road and crossed over the Kahalu'u Stream Bridge, capturing several shots of the Hygienic Store and the banyan tree. After he was done, he sat down between the roots and looked out at the street from where his brother might have also sat, adding another photograph to the collection: Kāne'ohe Bay, Mokoli'i barely visible in the distance. It gave him another idea.

By the time he got back, Mark had returned home from town, a used motor cradled in the bed of his truck. "How's it looking?" Elani asked him about the boat. Mark had been working diligently on making it seaworthy.

"Getting dea," Mark told him.

Elani walked over to the starboard side, where their brother had outlined a single word. Kāpaʻa, *to hold, as a canoe on its course*, Elani had searched out the definition the day after they had brought the boat home. "We should take it out," he told Mark. "When it's finished."

"Not going be fo one while," Mark said. "What about sku?"

What about it? he thought. "It can wait." He had more important stories to tell.

On the day of the celebration, he got to the church early. He had assembled several of the components at home, but he knew that the actual setting up would take him much of the morning. Rather than use the front of the hall, Elani decided to spread out the components, beginning at the front door and wrapping around the room. He had sections dedicated to Kāʻeo's childhood, to the family, to Kāʻeo's time in school, and after. Each section was a multi-modal mosaic, integrating extracts from Kāʻeo's journals, photographs that Elani had taken, and comments that Elani had gathered from those who were willing to share. Words were intertwined with images and recordings were spread throughout, tangling together to spring his brother to life.

"Stay so beautiful," Ma told Elani when she first entered the hall and saw all of the work that he had done.

"Just because he's not here, doesn't mean he's dead," Elani said, taking her hand and leading her around the room. They stopped at a picture from Kāʻeo's high school graduation, the whole family crammed into the shot: Tūtūpapa on one side of Kāʻeo, Pops on the other, all three holding the same stupid grin. "I want people to know that. I want people to know him."

Ma kissed Elani's forehead. "Your braddah would be proud."

The celebration lasted into the late afternoon. Elani talked with family that he had never been introduced to before, and heard about

Kāʻeo from people that his brother had met while in treatment, and from his brother's time on his own. A resident that had been in the same clinic as Kāʻeo pointed out several of the ʻōlelo noʻeau that Elani had used to mark off the sections and told him about how Kāʻeo had once led a group session. "He was always a positive tip, always there to support you but always knew when to let you know when you had a weak gut or when you had to get your shit together," the resident told Elani. "Pūpūkahi i holomua," he pointed out one of the proverbs. "After every session, everybody holding hands, pūpūkahi i holomua."

Under the proverb ʻAʻohe pau ka ʻike i ka hālau hoʻokahi, Elani included photographs that he had taken of the loʻi that Kāʻeo had tended and added in a recording of Jarrett explaining the moʻolelo of Hāloa-naka, the first ancestor of the Native Hawaiian people, and its relationship to kalo, the first plant of which grew from Hāloa-nakaʻs burial place. Elani wanted to emphasize that Kāʻeoʻs education came from more than just books. At one point during the celebration, Jarrett ended up posting himself up near the sprawl of stills that Elani had taken of the farm and stopping the tape to tell an anecdote about Kāʻeo. "I found him out there one morning, sleeping near the loʻi," Elani overheard Jarrett tell a neighbor. "He told me that he would go out there sometimes when he couldn't sleep. The sound of the leaves in the wind always cleared his mind."

After the party had emptied out, Elani walked over to the center of the room. He had set up a large poster board there with a picture of Kāʻeo when he was a kid, coming out of the water at Kualoa. On the table in front of it, one of his brother's notebooks was open. He picked up the pen that he had left there for anyone who wanted to write his brother a message and added his own just below that of his granduncle's wife. O ka makapō wale no ka mea hāpapa i ka pōuli, he wrote. I have a purpose. I have a family. I'm not alone.

Outside the hall, he found Mark parked in the grass near the graveyard, sitting on his tailgate. The sun was going down and his was one of the few vehicles that were left in the parking lot. "Was nice," Mark told Elani, moving over to give him space to sit. "I never even know we was related to half of these people."

"You think he would've liked it?" Elani asked, resting his body on the edge of the tailgate.

"What you think?"

"I think so," Elani looked back at the hall, a few bodies still lingering in conversation under the eaves. "He'd probably be spending most of the night out here though," he conceded.

"Kāʻeo was one simple guy, ah?" Mark noted. "Never one fo dis kine."

"Nope, he never even wanted a birthday party or anything."

"Nah, he jus like chill and talk story," Mark added. "All he wen need was good food and good company, you know?"

"We're all like that, I guess, yeah? The whole family."

Mark smirked. "Eh, I got to admit" he began. "Since you wen get back, you stay different. I almost no recognize you," Mark paused.

"What d'you mean?"

"You jus stay putting yourself out dea, you know? No reservations, no hibernation."

Elani nodded, "I guess so."

"And da shit you wen do in dea…" Mark shook his brother by the shoulders.

"You one real artist, you know dat?" Mark said, no hint of sarcasm in his voice, only approval.

"I think I just had something to say and I found a way to say it."

Mark nodded, "Shit was fucking unreal."

"You think so?"

"I think I never wen see you li'dat, so da kine, you know? I mean, I wen see so much passion in you. I never seen dat wen you was writing, not li'dis anyway."

Elani agreed. "I felt like he was with me, you know that?" he said to Mark. "The whole time, I felt like he was guiding me along."

"He was always one fo give orders," Mark cracked a smile.

"Especially with you," Elani threw in, nudging him in his side.

"He was one asshole sometimes," Mark crossed his arms. "But we was kids, ah? Braddahs li'dat."

"Yeah, you were worse."

"Fuck you," Mark punched his shoulder and hopped down from the truck. "We go clean up and get out of hea already."

"Actually," Elani stopped him before he could disappear. "I wanted to talk to you about something, see what you thought."

"About what?"

"About his ashes," Elani answered. It had been on his mind since he had visited the banyan tree. "About what to do with them."

"Going sit up on da hutch, jus like wit Papa's, jus like wit Pops."

"I don't think that's what he'd want, to be confined and boxed in," Elani reasoned. "I think when the boat's ready, we should take it out one night—"

"And what?"

"And return him to the water, a place he always felt like he belonged," Elani finished. "Mokoliʻi, what d'you think?"

Mark fell back against his truck. "Stay dangerous, Elani," Mark objected. "We better off walking across da reef bumbai we get stuck out dea or worse."

"Since when are you scared?" Elani challenged him.

"Since wen you not?" Mark pushed back.

"Just think about it," Elani continued his proposal. "You're almost done right? We can map it out, take the boat for a few test runs, and learn the water."

"And den what?"

"And then when we're ready, we head out there just before dawn and we have one last race," Elani replied with a passion that made his body tremble.

Mark bowed his head and took a moment to consider Elani's suggestion. It didn't take him long to make up his mind. He wiped his face and looked up. "One last race," Mark nodded, agreeing that it was exactly what their brother would want.

It would be several more weeks before the boat was ready, but Elani and Mark worked on it every day, replacing the floorboards and the riser, and then the seats. They mounted the motor and installed the fuel line, and then took to fastening the cleats to the gunwale. They used the how-to guide that Elani had found in Kāʻeo's things, and consulted with one of their neighbors who had built and restored boats for most of his life. It was a large undertaking, but Elani found a certain joy in the process, finding small reminders of Kāʻeo's efforts throughout: tick marks and measurements, notes in the margins of the guide; and it also gave Elani a chance to connect with Mark in a way that he had never connected with him before, through action and cooperation, through the experience that they were sharing side-by-side.

When they weren't working on the boat, they were looking over a chart of the bay or talking with fisherman at the pier, where they had met a boat captain who offered to take them out on the ocean. Elani learned the placement of the channel markers and memorized the distance between them. They went out at night and learned just how difficult it was going to be, but each time, they became more and more familiar with the water, until finally they felt comfortable enough to go out on their own.

They waited until after New Year's Day, when the full moon would be out and visibility would be best. Elani spent the afternoon going over the route again, while Mark checked the motor, the safety vests, and made sure that they had paddles just in case they needed them. After dinner, they packed Kāʻeo's ashes, portioning the remains into two separate plastic bags.

At four a.m., Elani and Mark piled into Mark's truck. They drove over the Kahaluʻu Stream Bridge, past the Hygienic Store, and made a left turn, following Kamehameha Highway. They continued on the road, passing the spot where their father had crashed, not stopping until they pulled into Heʻeia Kea Pier. Elani got out of the truck and helped Mark down the ramp and then helped him to free the boat from the trailer. Elani started the engine while Mark parked the truck, and then they headed out on the water.

They were careful to keep to the main channel. Mark avoided the reef while Elani watched the shadowed depths. The moon was hidden behind a bright veil of gray, the light still fell over the ocean in pale stretches, making their path forward clear. When they could make out the strip of sand where the islet split, Mark cut the engine and let the current guide the hull until they were close enough to anchor, Elani hopping out to make sure that the boat was secure.

On the shore, Elani walked up to a spot that faced Kualoa Beach. He looked back at the silhouette of the world that they had left behind and couldn't help but appreciate the quiet. He could hear the breeze, but more than that, he could feel his body pulsing in his ears, echoing with the movement of the waves. He understood now why their brother had been drawn there. Elani could feel its presence in his marrow.

Elani turned back and crossed the sand, climbing up to meet Mark. His brother was waiting for him near a cluster of black rock that protruded up from the ocean, the waves churning below. Elani crouched down and looked out at the ocean. The water was rougher here, deeper.

"I wouldn't have made it," Elani remarked, thinking about how his brothers used to race out to the island when they were kids. "Not out here, not by myself."

"Was some close calls," Mark looked down at his right arm, the scar lost to the hour. "But out hea, we was never alone, ah?"

Elani nodded. "I took that for granted," he licked his lips, tasting the salt air. "All these years."

"No need fo tell me," Mark admitted, stepping out to the edge. "But not tonight," he added. "Not anymore."

They waited until the waves had settled and a thin division of light was on the horizon, with dawn blooming the color of hala flowers. Mark unzipped his backpack and handed one of the bags to his brother. Elani ran his thumb across the plastic, smoothing down the ashes, still not ready to believe that their brother was really gone. "Stay time," he told Elani.

Elani nodded. "Together," he said.

"Fo Kā'eo," Mark added. "Fo Tūtū papa, fo Pops."

"For all of us," Elani said, and then put the bag between his teeth and slipped down into the water.

The waves broke against their bones, each one trying to push them back before gently pulling them deeper. Elani kept to Mark's wake until he found the rhythm of the current, and then he shot forward and closed the gap. Elani didn't know how far out they were going, and he didn't care; all that mattered now was that they got there. They swam further and further out, until somewhere between sky and sea, they felt their brother beside them, and in that moment, they dove.

Acknowledgments

I would like to thank my love, my partner, and my first editor, Danielle Lanakila Carreira Ching. Much of what made its way to the page came about through our discussions, debates, and late night car rides. She has never wavered in her support of my writing and has always made sure to share her ideas and to take the time to help me work through my own, even when that meant having to listen to me obsess over the smallest details over and over again. She is a constant inspiration and without her this novel would never have been written. For that and more, I owe her everything.

A great deal of thanks to Darrell and Eric, whose insight and patience helped to shape a conceptual mass of characters and ideas into a story of three brothers and their family's struggle to persevere. It's been a chaotic and stressful two years, but their efforts on this project have always remained steadfast. I am humbled by the opportunity to share this story, and without them would not have had the chance to. I would also like to thank the entire Bamboo Ridge family: Joy, Wing Tek, Lisa, Rowen, Gail, Marie, Juliet, Jean, Peter, Misty, Kent, and Micheline. I don't know how you folks do what you do, but you do, and for that I am grateful.

I would also like to thank those that influenced my writing and guided me as a student. Craig Howes, for teaching me about the complexities of story, the importance of thorough research, and for never hesitating to review my latest draft. Rodney Morales, for shaping my understanding of character development and the importance of structure. Morgan Blair, for teaching me that writing is a process and a discipline. I would also like to thank Cristina Bacchilega, Candace Fujikane, and Kuʻualoha Hoʻomanawanui for teaching me what it means to write about Hawaiʻi and the responsibility that comes with writing stories about Hawaiʻi. Special thanks as well to Ranjan Adiga, Bonnie Fujii, M. Thomas Gammarino, Jaimie Guzman, Jody Helfand, Uzma Khan, David Maine, David Milks, Georganne Nordstrom, Gary Pak, Mark Panek, and Alan Ragains for their support, encouragement, and feedback over the years. In addition, I would like to thank my fellow writers for sharing their perspectives and thoughts with me: Amalia Bueno, Donovan Kūhiō Colleps, Kapena Landgraf, Doug Neagoy, Cheri Nagashima, Alexei Melnick, Chris Nelson, Sam Pastore-Braden, and Kevin Won.

A large thanks to my family on both sides. My father and my mother for raising me right, reading to me early, and sending me to public school. Natalie, for the love that you always showed me even when I couldn't see it. Louis, for letting me "borrow" your shoes and sharing a room with me. Grandpa and Grandma for being there always. Grandma Josie for guava jelly. Elani and Dana, for your unconditional love, for talking story, and for showing me how to make laulau. Nicole, for being a true friend and sister. I would also like to thank Kāʻeo, Mark, Reid, and Wade, for all of those crazy years we spent on the wall, on the corner, or in the back of pickup trucks. Aunty Carol and Uncle Mel for always leaving the screen door open.

Finally, a great deal of thanks is owed to the writers, researchers, scholars, and artists whose own work informed my writing of this novel, especially to the great Mary Kawena Pukui for *Nānā I Ke Kumu* (*Look to the Source*) Vol. 1 and 2, *ʻŌlelo Noʻeau: Hawaiian Proverbs and Poetical Sayings*, and *Place Names of Hawaiʻi*. Also, thank you to the following for their work: Pierre Bourdieu, Samuel H. Elbert, Antonio Gramsci, Michael Haas, Kuʻualoha Hoʻomanawanui, Thomas King, Anne Kapulani Landgraf, Seri Luangphinith, Karl Marx, Jonathan Kay Kamakawiwoʻole Osorio, and Haunani-Kay Trask. I would also like to thank kumu hula Kaʻohu Cazinha, and Bryan Kuwada for aiding me with my inquires.

Donald Carreira Ching was born and raised in Kahaluʻu. He graduated with his BA in English and his MA in Creative Writing from the University of Hawaiʻi at Mānoa, where he also received the Myrtle Clark Award with distinction and the Sumie Saiki Award for Fiction. His short stories have appeared in numerous publications and anthologies locally and elsewhere, including *Bamboo Ridge*, *Hawaiʻi Review*, *Rio Grande Review*, and on the radio program, *Aloha Shorts*. In 2012, he was selected as the runner-up in the *Honolulu Weekly* fiction competition, was selected as the winner in the *Honolulu Star-Advertiser*'s Halloween Fiction contest, and was voted the Best Writer in Pidgin 2012 in *Honolulu Weekly*'s "Best of Honolulu." In 2014, he won the Ian MacMillan Award for Fiction. He currently lives and teaches on Oʻahu.